ELIZA SCALIA

Chasing the Sprinter

The Adventures of Silver Dove, Book Three

Eliza Scalia

Cover Illustration by:
Cheyanne and Jean Buffkin
Based upon the characters originally
designed by Suji Gallianetti

ISBN:978-1947523760

Dedicated to Jean Buffkin, who helped name a few of my characters over the years and has provided endless encouragement in my writing career from the very beginning. I wouldn't be where I am without her. There are no sufficient words in this language that can explain my gratitude to her.

Contents

Chapter One

Colomba-Monsters

Flying through the air as Silver Dove, I slash my sword at a massive lizard like hand that tries to trap me in its grasp. Its claws only just miss me, I can feel the wind rush past me from the force of its huge hand. Standing on the ground beneath me is a huge monstrous lizard that almost reminds me of Godzilla. It roars up in frustration at me, furious that it can't reach me this high up. The force of its roar sends me flying higher into the air. I gag at the smell of its disgusting breath. It almost smells like a dog's breath, only about a hundred times worse. It is another one of the creatures that the Crow has created, a poor soul from my school who he has tricked into giving superpowers so that they can create mayhem and destruction all throughout my school.

The Crow stands off to the side, watching all of this with an evil smile of joy on his face at seeing me struggle to fight his new monster. I have already been fighting this creature for a long time. I can barely even hold my sword up anymore since I am so tired. My strength fails me, and I can no longer fly. Falling back down to earth, I crash on top of some debris that we had created during our fight. I moan in agony, wanting nothing more than to just go home and sleep, but I am not allowed that luxury. The monster picks me up from the wreck, its giant hand wrapping around my entire body. I am too tired to try and fight my way out of its grasp. My body hangs limply in the massive hand that holds me.

The monster holds me tight in its grip holding me high in the air. I struggle for air, trying to breathe in its tight grip while the Crow laughs as he flies up to stand on the shoulder of the monster.

"How do you like my newest creation Silver Dove?" He chuckles coldly as he listens to me moan in pain as the monster tightens its grip around me. The Crow's smile grows bigger as he turns to his monster and gives it an order. "Eat her." The monster growls as it opens its huge mouth to reveal long, sharp teeth. I scream in horror as it brings me closer and closer to its mouth while the Crow keeps laughing. All I see is the darkness inside the monster's mouth before I open my eyes, gasping for breath in terror. I am laying down in bed, holding my blankets in a tight grip as sweat pours down my face. Of course, it was just a dream.

I feel tears beginning to form in my eyes. Every night for almost four months, ever since I first met the Crow, I have been having nightmares about him. I feel so pathetic, and not to mention tired. It really takes a lot out of you having constant nightmares every single night. I have already defeated this guy twice, yet I am still terrified of him. How can I be afraid of someone I've already beaten? It's just so stupid. How can I be so stupid?

Not wanting anyone in my house to hear me cry, I go into the shower and let myself cry there, my sobs being masked by the sound of falling water. I cry to let out my frustration and confusion about this entire situation. Sometimes it feels nice to let everything out in one good cry. I only give myself ten minutes to cry it out before I force myself to stop and get out of the shower to head down to breakfast. When I get down to the kitchen, my grandma has finished making breakfast and my dad is already eating his waffles while reading the morning paper. I give him a quick kiss on the cheek as I sit down in my seat beside Grandma, who gives me a waffle and passes the syrup to me with her usual warm smile on her face. I smile back at her, not wanting to worry her with what I am going through right now.

Grandma doesn't know about the nightmares I've been having every night, and I never want her to find out. I don't want to worry her. She is the one who gave me my powers, I don't want her to feel bad about turning me into Silver Dove. I love my new powers, and I don't want her to try and take them away from me just because of these nightmares. Even though I love my powers she would take them from me if she thought that it would be for my best interests. All I need to do is just keep going, eventually these nightmares will go away, I just need to wait until then. I can only hope that this will happen soon or else I am going to start falling asleep in class because I am so tired.

"Will you look at that." My dad says under his breath as he carefully examines a page in the paper.

"Look at what?" I ask as I cut up my syrup covered waffle. Dad turns his paper around so that I can see the front page of the sports section where a picture of a girl a year or two older than me is running on the school track field.

"Apparently a girl from your school's track team is taking the team to nationals this year. This girl, Cheyanne Bulkin, apparently won first in almost every category during their last competition. The coach says that she is probably the best runner the school has ever had." I look closer at the picture and I suddenly recognize her.

"Oh yeah, I know her. She's in my gym class."

During gym, no matter what we are doing, the gym teacher lets her do laps instead so that she can practice. In the photo she is running past the finish line for a track meet, decked out in her track team uniform. A red T-shirt with the school mascot, the Drew's Hollow Horseman, printed in black on the front. Beneath that she has on black shorts with red leggings coming out from underneath. A huge smile is on her face in the picture as she lifts up both of her hands in the air in her triumph as she wins first place.

Cheyanne is a junior and is extremely popular. Everyone looks up to her. Since she has brought our school so many trophies from her track meets, she has kind of become the school hero. Because of her amazing running skills, she has been given the nickname the Sprinter. Despite her success and popularity though, she is nice to everyone and hasn't picked on anybody like I have heard a lot of the popular kids do. No matter what, she is always willing to help someone and gives them a reassuring smile whenever they are feeling low. I don't know her very well, but I am sure that she would be happy to make friends with me, or anybody who wants to be friends with her. Sometimes it is hard to tell, but I can easily see that she has a good heart. You can just see the goodness inside her when you look into her eyes.

"Maybe we should get tickets for nationals. I

would love to see if she's as great as everyone says she is." My dad says this with his usual smile, and I know instantly that even though he said we *might* go, we are definitely going. I smile back at him with excitement making my heart leap in my chest.

"Yeah, I would like that. It sounds like a ton of fun. I can't wait." We all finish our waffles before my dad leaves for work and I head out to our mailbox to wait for the bus.

Now that I am alone at the mailbox, I think about my nightmares. Closing my eyes, I rub my hands against my face, trying to rub the sleepiness from my features. I have no idea how I am alive right now with how little sleep I've been getting recently. Before all of this started, I would sleep around eight hours a night just like doctors always say you should, but recently I have only been getting around four or five hours of sleep a night. Sometimes I am so tired that it feels like I am walking in my sleep during the day. Sometimes I am afraid that I may fall asleep at a bad moment and get hurt. I can't sleep because of those stupid nightmares.

The other night I had a nightmare where the Crow turned another student into something that looked like a werewolf and it ripped me apart with its teeth. The night before that I had a nightmare where he had an army of zombies that took over the school. And the night before that I had a nightmare where he turned someone into something that looked like a giant eagle with a lion for a head, that dream was particularly weird. Every night there is always a nightmare, every night I wake up terrified, and every morning I wake up exhausted because of those dreams.

Even though the details of each dream are different, the same basic thing happens in each one. The Crow gives somebody superpowers, that person terrifies everybody, I try to fight them as Silver Dove, I lose, and then I get destroyed by the Crow's minion in a really gross or scary way. The only real differences between these dreams is what kind of powers the Crow gives them, what part of the school the fight takes place in, and how I get destroyed. I have no idea what I am going to about these nightmares, but I know that I have to do something soon or else I will go nuts from lack of sleep.

The bus pulls up over the hill, its breaks squealing as it stops in front of my mailbox. I get on and head immediately to the seat I always sit in and wait a few minutes before my friend Nat is picked up, and then a stop or two later, our other friend Luis comes on. He smiles warmly as soon as he sees the two of us.

I am honestly worried about Luis. He is a big supporter of the Crow, and I am worried that he might make the wrong decision because of his loyalty to a monster like the Crow. If the Crow were to ask his followers to do something for him, I am afraid that Luis will do it without any questions.

Even though the two of us know that we support different people, him with the Crow and me with Silver Dove, we never talk about it anymore because we know that it will lead to an argument. I feel bad knowing that I can easily get into an argument with one of my best friends over something so big, but I know that I can't change it. His loyalty to the Crow is one reason why I have never told him about my nightmares. He would think it's silly to be so afraid of someone he thinks of as a hero, and then he would try to convince me to join his side again. I don't want to go through that argument again, so I stay silent. I don't want to risk losing one of my best friends over something like that.

The three of us talk casually, laughing at each other's jokes while I am having trouble just keeping my eyes open. It doesn't take us long to make it to the school and I gladly hop off to start my day. Stepping off the bus among the crowd of other students, I see a familiar face and I can't help but smile. Jade Elizabeth, who had been transformed into Tigerclaw a little over two months ago by the Crow, is now walking beside a girl from my English class, listening to the girl tell her a story. Jade Elizabeth had been so shy that she could barely speak to anybody and didn't have any friends, now she has a few friends and is starting to come out of her shell more. It feels as if my feet have left the ground, I am so happy to see that she is getting better. Even though I feel awful from having so little sleep and one of my best friends hates me as Silver Dove, at least I know that somebody's life has improved because of me. That's at least one thing to feel happy about when everything else looks so dark.

The three of us head into the school to get to our first class. My feet practically drag across the floor as I do so. I'm too tired to lift my feet as I walk. When I sit down at my desk in first period, I have to fight myself to keep my eyes open as class starts. The teacher keeps talking, and I use all of my strength to pay attention, trying to do anything to stay awake. As I try harder and harder to listen, the teacher's voice just seems to get farther and farther away from me. I take notes about the lesson while I try to hold back the horrible memory of the nightmare I had last night that keeps trying to invade my mind. I shudder at the thought of that terrible monster since I know that the Crow might create something just like it soon enough.

Chapter Two

Luis-
No Change

As I step off the bus, I have to hide a scowl of misery from my friends. I don't want them to see my disappointment and pain. I have had these powers for over four months now, but not much has really changed in my school. Despite the fact that everyone knows that I am here to get rid of all the bullying at my school, people are still picking on each other. I hear people calling each other terrible things for no reason, people spread rumors on A-Streamer (a popular social media site in our town), and I even heard about how one kid got beaten up after school some time last week for some reason, but I can probably guess it was for something stupid since he is one of the kids that gets bullied constantly just like me. When a bullied kid gets beaten up, it's usually for a reason that doesn't make much sense, usually just because the person who beats them up is bored. The other students in my school act as if what I did with Tigerclaw didn't happen at all. It doesn't make sense! How stupid are these people that they can still pick on each other even though I have warned them that I will come back as the Crow to make them pay for it if they keep doing this? These people who go to school with me don't make any sense at all. Maybe that's why they pick on me, I'm the only one that can see sense and they hate me for it.

While I am walking up to the school, I notice someone that I recognize, Jade Elizabeth, Tigerclaw, my first soldier. She is talking to someone as they also head into the school to start the day. I smile when I look at her. At least one person is doing better in their life because of me. I gave her powers and she used it to fight back. Even though Silver Dove stopped her in the end, I think that her time as Tigerclaw helped give her the strength to stop being as shy as she was before. She was so painfully shy before that she could barely talk to people, now she is making friends. She is making friends because of me. I can only hope that she will never forget what I have done for her as the Crow.

I separate from Colomba and Nat so that I can head to my first period. While I am walking, I keep my head down. I am trying not to be seen by anybody, but I can't hide from them all. Someone throws something at the back of my head while I hear them shouting mean things. I try not to pay attention though as I keep walking, trying to ignore the pain on the back of my head. This doesn't stop another person from joining in the fun of picking on me. Alex walks up behind me and wraps his arm around my shoulder.

"Hey there Louie. How are you doin' today?" Even though his words are polite, his tone tells me that he doesn't care how I feel, he doesn't care about me at all. From his tone I can already tell that he wants something from me. "I was hoping I would run into you Louie. You see I haven't finished my assignment for class today, I was hoping I could copy off you before I turn mine in. A nerd like you always finishes his homework." He says this sarcastically and I know that he isn't saying this as a request, it is a demand. A demand that has very bad consequences if I don't do as he says.

Before I got my Crow Medal, I would have probably given my assignment to him without a second thought. I would be terrified of not giving it to him since I knew that he would hurt me, but now I am thinking about things differently. I don't want to give it to him, he didn't do his assignment so he should get what he deserves. He should get a bad grade for not doing his work. Plus, I don't even like him, so I don't want to do him any kind of favor. Knowing that I have power has given me strength even without using my medal. I feel more confident to do what I have in mind. I look at Alex and glare at him.

"No. I'm not giving it to you." I say this in a growl that makes him move slightly away from me in surprise. Alex stares at me with complete shock. His eyes look over my face, probably trying to figure out if he heard me correctly. He isn't used to me standing up for myself, but he's going to have to get used to it because I'm not going to stand for it anymore. His look of surprise quickly changes into a glare of rage.

"You might want to change your mind Louie, or else things might get pretty ugly for you very soon. You should know by now that I don't like it when I don't get what I want." I know that I shouldn't take his threat lightly, but I walk away from him with a glare to match his. I am so totally going to get beat up after school for that. I walk away from him quickly and head straight for the classroom and practically fall into my seat. My heart is beating like crazy in my chest from my fear. It feels like I have just finished running a marathon. I guess that even though I have stood up for myself, I am still afraid of Alex. I feel like such a wimp. I have superpowers, why I am still afraid of Alex?

As I sit and wait for the teacher to start the class, Alex makes his way into the classroom with a scowl on his face. I can tell from his angry expression that he couldn't find anyone else to copy their homework. He gives me a venomous glare before he smacks the back of my head with the back of his hand while heading to his own seat. I'm not surprised that the teacher didn't say anything about this even though I'm pretty sure that they saw what happened. Instead of helping me they just start the class while my head throbs.

Why do the teachers never say anything about all the kids getting picked on? I know that they see what happens most of the time, so why don't they do something about it? They could get Alex in trouble for what he's doing. I know that he does stuff like this all the time, not just to me, but to other people as well, so why is nothing done? I look around at the other students and I see a few of them look away from me as soon as I lock eyes with them. They saw what happened too, but they are ignoring me just like the teacher. Can't they see that I am in pain, why won't they help me? They are afraid too. They don't want to get picked on like me so they stay silent. Either that or they just don't care about the people getting picked on like me. How can they all be so heartless?

I guess that this is why I have lost hope that anybody will help me. I have to help myself as the

Crow so that I can stop people like him. If Alex becomes so afraid of the Crow giving bullied kids superpowers to get revenge on him, then he will stop. Deep down, he is probably a wimp too, so he will just quit if I scare him enough. I find myself smiling at that thought. I can't wait to see Alex letting his true colors show when he begs me for forgiveness.

The class ends pretty quickly for me and I run out of the room so that Alex won't be able to catch up to me. I know that if he catches me, I am dead meat. My second class of the day passes quickly for me too since I am still scared to death, knowing that Alex will be in my fourth class and I can't possibly avoid him then. The only thing that makes my second class tolerable is Colomba who sits next to me, telling me a funny story about her grandparents. Even though she is cheering me up, since she somehow could figure out that I am upset, she looks as if she is about to collapse in her chair and fall asleep on the ground.

Has she slept at all recently? I'm a bit worried about her. She has looked like this for a while. Dark circles haunt underneath her eyes and her movements are slower, like a zombie. She has just been lacking her usual happy energy. I don't know what could be keeping her up. I can only hope that this will pass. If she is going through anything bad, I want to help her. It pains me to see her like this and I want to see her as her usual happy self again.

I groan in misery when the bell rings, telling me that I have to face Alex soon in my fourth class. Walking beside Colomba, we chat casually as we leave the room to head to our next classes. While I listen to her, I look at her face, unable to get enough. I could stare at her forever, but that's a bit creepy by anyone's standards so I can't do that. She smiles innocently as I tell her a funny story that my uncle has told me about when he and my parents were moving to this country from Puerto Rico. Too bad this moment can't last forever. Eventually we have to go our separate ways so that we can go to our different classes.

Passing through the hallways, I want to just disappear. I want to leave this place and never come back. I walk through the halls knowing that I am a dead man walking. As soon as Alex has me alone he will beat me up mercilessly for not giving him my homework. I can only wait for the disaster to come. I can only wait patiently for my doom.

Chapter Three

Colomba-
The Missing
Hero

Stepping out of the girl's locker room in my gym shorts and T- shirt, I make my way over to the center of the gym where everyone else is waiting for the coach to start class. It doesn't take very long for Alex to join me. When I look at him, I have to admit that he is very handsome. He is rather tall, not as tall as Luis though, and has light brown hair that hangs over his forehead yet stays out of his eyes so that the dark green in his eyes can clearly be seen. He has liked me ever since we met, he hasn't made that hard to figure out, but I don't think that I will ever date him. Alex is very nice to me, but he doesn't seem to be kind to other people. I never really see him do anything to other people, but it's the way everyone acts around him that makes me think this way. They either avoid him like he is a cranky bear, or they are trying to make him happy, not because they like him, but because they are afraid of what might happen if they disappoint him. I don't understand what kind of power he holds over everyone, but I know that I don't want to get close enough to him to find out. I am fine with just being friends with him. I want to remain friends with him since he is kind to me and it would be rude to not be friendly to him since he has never shown me any unkindness, but we will never be anything more than that. Even though Alex wants to date me, I will never do that.

The other students chatter around us as I silently watch them while Alex talks about something that I am honestly not really paying much attention to. As I glance around at the other students in the class, I notice that one person is missing.

"That's strange, Cheyanne is missing today. She never misses school." That is true, she never misses school because she never wants to miss track practice after school. She also enjoys coming to school from what I can tell. It's always nice to go to a place where you are considered a hero by everyone. Alex looks around at the crowd around us to see that I am right.

"Huh, that is weird. I guess she's just sick today or something." I shake my head, starting to feel a bit worried.

"I really hope not. Nationals is only a week or so away and I don't want her to try and push herself when she still isn't feeling well. That would only make it worse for her." Cheyanne does seem like the kind of girl who would still go and try to compete at nationals even if she does still feel a bit sick. She is the kind of person who just won't give up on what she wants, even if something like an illness stands in her way. It's a trait she has that can be admired, yet still isn't quite the best thing for her.

"Oh, she'll be fine." Alex says as if this is nothing, as if he doesn't care about Cheyanne's condition at all. I stare at him for a moment as he continues to talk. I try to see if I can find any concern for Cheyanne on his face, but I don't see anything. I try to ignore that as the coach comes up to everyone to say that we will be doing laps today in celebration for our track team going to nationals.

As we all begin to run, I have a strange thought that nags me. It almost feels like Alex is glad that Cheyanne is gone today. People have been talking about the track team going to nationals nonstop for weeks and he seems to be annoyed by it, but also a bit jealous. I think that he's jealous that the girl's track team is getting talked about so much when the football and basketball teams are the ones everyone usually talks about. Both teams he is a part of.

Alex seems to be the kind of guy who always wants to be the center of attention, whether the attention is good or bad. Whenever we talk, he somehow always gets the conversation turned to him. He always has to talk about himself. It's almost as if nothing else really matters to him, well except me. He seems to care for me quite a bit too. He always wants to be near me and loves to talk to me, but when he does talk to me, he is always showing off somehow. He is always showing off about his athleticism, his family's money, or how popular he is. Alex is always so nice to me, but I want him to be able to see that there is more to life than just himself. I want to help him be a better person, but I know that I can't change him. Even though I know that I can't change him, I don't want to stop being his friend.

Alex and I are leading the group of runners, and he talks constantly as we run while my mind wanders. I'm not sure why, but I am worried about Cheyanne. I know that she's probably just at home sick or something, but something in the back of my mind is telling me that something terrible has happened. Something has happened to her and it will lead to something horrible. I close my eyes for a moment to get rid of this terrible thought. I'm making a mountain out of a mole hill, that's what my dad would tell me. I'm getting worried over nothing and I'm stressing myself out for no reason at all. Everything is just fine.

We keep running until the coach tells us that it is time to shower before class ends. I shower quickly and change back into my normal clothes, a white skirt with a pale blue blouse. As Alex and I leave the gym while the bell rings loudly around us, I see him pull a soda out of his backpack. Kinda strange for him to drink a soda so early in the morning, but I don't ask him about it. I don't want to seem nosy. The hallway is already crowded when we walk out of the gym and the two of us join the crowd. While I pass through the hallways a familiar feeling comes over me, the feeling as if something terrible is about to happen. What is going to happen? This feeling is telling me that it has something to do with Alex, but I don't know what. We separate to go to our next classes, but my worry follows Alex. I can only hope that nothing bad will happen to him. As I think this, a small voice in the back of my mind speaks up. It warns me that what I feel will happen won't happen *to* Alex, it will happen *because* of him.

I scold myself in my head. I can't think that way about someone I consider a friend. What's wrong with me? How could I think that about Alex when he hasn't done anything to make me think that he would do something awful? I shake my head, ashamed at myself while I keep walking through the crowd to get to my next class. You should never think like that about anyone. Thinking they will do something bad just because of a feeling you have without any evidence is just terrible. I could never do that to a friend.

Chapter Four

Luis-
Escape

When the end of class bell rings my heart is doing summersaults in my chest. Alex is going to do something to me I just know it. I make it to the art room and breathe a sigh of relief. Alex isn't here yet, but the teacher is. This means that he can't do anything to me without Mr. Sizemore noticing, and Mr. Sizemore is the kind of teacher that actually cares if one of his students is picking on another. This is one of the many reasons why he is my favorite teacher. He will make sure that nothing will happen to me. I am safe as long as he is here.

Sitting down in my spot, I take out my sketchbook and start working on our assignment. Right now, we are studying how to draw trees. Mr. Sizemore had written down a bunch of different types of trees on little slips of paper and placed them in a bowl. All of the students had to pick one of these slips and draw the type of tree written on their slip. I guess he did this since in our last assignment, drawing birds, everyone chose the same kinds of birds, either a crow or a dove. He just wants us all to draw something different. I chose an oak tree.

In my sketch, I have an oak tree standing tall in the center of a large field, the sun beginning to rise over the horizon. Right now, I am drawing a crow flying over the tree. It looks so majestic flying in the center of the rising sun. I smile as I draw the rays of light coming from the rising sun. It looks so real that I can almost feel the warmth of the sun coming from the drawing.

I am so absorbed in what I am doing that I don't notice an unwelcome person getting close to me, but I do notice what they do to me. A large stream of soda pours on top of my drawing, absolutely soaking my paper. I look up to see Alex holding a now empty can of soda in his hand, an evil smile on his face.

"Oh, I'm sorry Louie. I didn't mean to do that." He says his apology with so much sarcasm that it would be impossible to think that he really meant it. Glancing back, I can see that Mr. Sizemore has his back turned to us, helping another student with their drawing of a pine tree. He didn't see anything that Alex did. I glare up at Alex, wanting to do something, but I don't want to make it worse. I've already angered him once today, making him angrier won't help me. So instead of lashing out at him or saying something to him, I just glare at him in silence as he walks back to his seat with a triumphant smirk on his face. He gets a high five from a few of his friends who praise him for what he did to me. None of them even look the least bit sad for me. They enjoy watching my misery.

Looking down at my drawing, I can see that it's ruined. The soda has made the drawing disappear into a brown mess of cola and soggy paper. I close my eyes tightly to prevent myself from crying. I know that I shouldn't cry, I don't want to look like a wimp, but I feel so helpless. Nobody can or will help me. The other students won't help, the teachers won't help, *I* can't even help myself. Why won't anyone help me?

When Mr. Sizemore sees what happened I just tell him that I spilled some soda on it and I will get started on it again. It didn't look like he believed me when I told him that it had been an accident, but he didn't argue with me. I can't tell him now about what Alex did or Alex would make sure that my beating will be worse than what he already has planned for being a snitch. The final bell is ringing now, and I have most of my sketch finished again. It is almost completely the same as the one that had been ruined, but there is one major difference.

Instead of having the crow flying in the center of a bright, warm sunrise, the crow is now flying over a dark, cold moon. The drawing has lost all of its warmth. When I look at it now, I feel a shiver go through my stomach. When I look at it now, I feel miserable.

I pick up my stuff quickly and run out of the room, not wanting to give Alex the chance to catch up with me and try something else. The day seems to fly by after that, not giving me enough time to figure out a way to avoid Alex when school ends. Even if I did have more time, I probably couldn't think of anything. I have never really been the best at finding ways of avoiding Alex even though I have had plenty of practice over the years. I guess I will just have to make something up on the fly.

As I follow the crowd of students making their way to the front doors where the buses wait outside, I keep my eyes peeled for a certain unfriendly face. From the corner of my eye I see Alex leaning against a wall near the front doors, carefully scanning the crowd, looking for someone. I know that he is looking for me. He wants revenge on me since I didn't let him copy my homework earlier this morning. I know what will happen, things like this have happened to me before. Whenever I have done something that Alex doesn't like he finds me after school and beats me up or does something awful to embarrass me. I need to do something right now to make sure that he won't do something to me. What can I do to escape when he's only ten feet away from me?

Looking around, I try to come up with a plan. I know that I can't leave those doors without him seeing me, so I need to come up with something to make him not want to come near me. Glancing behind myself, I smile when I see someone who will fix this situation, my guardian angel, Colomba. Walking up to her, I start walking by her side.

"Hey Colomba, how has your day been?" She smiles warmly at me.

"It's been a good day for me, how about you?" I smile back down at her.

"Fantastic." We both leave through the front doors, right past Alex. He glares at me furiously, angry that I have ruined his plans again. I know that he will never do anything bad to me in front of Colomba. He has a crush on her and doesn't want her to see him as the monster I think of him as. She gives him a simple wave as we walk past him, while he gives her a half- hearted smile and waves back while silently waving a fist at me as soon as Colomba has turned her back to him. Being the idiot that I am, I smirk at him as he waves his fists. This only makes his eyes grow wide in shock before narrowing into thin slits. His hands hang at his side in tight, angry fists. I am definitely going to pay for that later, but for now I enjoy my small victory.

Colomba and I make it to the bus while happiness and fear makes my stomach churn while I wonder what will happen to me. I feel happiness since I got away from Alex this time yet fear as well since I know that this won't be his last attempt to get me. The bus ride doesn't last very long, and I make it to my uncle's shop in no time. When I walk in the front door, Uncle Diego is talking with a customer, so I head upstairs to the apartment that we share. Walking into my room, I lock the door behind me before I place my hand over my medal and Shadow appears on my dresser.

"Hello Master, how are you?" She actually seems glad to see me. For a while now she has been pretty upset with me. She's a bit disappointed in how I've been using my powers. I want to give bullied kids superpowers so that they can fight back, so that they can get revenge. I am doing this so that I can end the bullying at my school. Shadow doesn't understand this though. She agrees with Silver Dove and thinks that I should stop this, but recently she has been acting more friendly with me. I guess she feels that, since she is stuck with me as her master, she might as well get used to the idea and make the most of it.

"I'm not doing alright to be honest." She nods her head at me.

"Yes, I know. I was just trying to be polite by asking." I can't help but smile at that.

"Thanks." She chuckles softly.

"You're welcome. I'm sorry about what Alex did to your drawing." I look away from her, not wanting her to see the pain in my eyes.

"It's alright, he has done worse to me before." Shadow can sense my discomfort with this conversation, so she thankfully changes the subject.

"You have made yourself quiet as the Crow for a while now. You barely even talk about your plans anymore. What has caused this change in you?" I suddenly feel a bit angry by her words. I think she already knows the answer to that question. Not too long ago, I tried to start my plan as the Crow by giving a bullied kid, a girl named Jade Elizabeth, superpowers. I turned her into Tigerclaw so that she could get revenge on her bullies who picked on her because she was so shy that she could barely speak to anyone. She had been doing so well, then Silver Dove came along and ruined everything. Silver Dove convinced Tigerclaw to stop fighting, telling her that everything would be alright and the dummy actually believed her! I lost that fight because Silver Dove outsmarted Tigerclaw and me, but I won't let that happen again! I can't let it happen again!

I let my anger fade away so that I won't upset Shadow by yelling at her. She has only just started acting nicer to me, I don't want to end that already.

"I am being more cautious. I don't want to make the same mistakes as I did with Tigerclaw.

Tigerclaw was my first soldier and she failed. I want to make sure that my second soldier won't be such a disappointment. I need to be more careful this time." Shadow sighs softly as she nods her head.

"I understand. I can only hope that you make the right decision." Something in the back of my mind is telling me that she isn't saying that she wants me to make the "right decision" about choosing my next soldier. She's hoping that I make the "right decision" and end my plan and join up with Silver Dove instead. She has told me a million times that she and I are supposed to be a team to defeat evil and blah, blah, blah, bla- blah, but I have other plans. I will end the bullying at my school with force, because that's the only way I will be able to make everyone understand. That's the only way they'll listen to what I have to say. People don't really listen when other people talk. They hear the words, but they don't listen. They don't pay attention to what is trying to be said. That's why you have to use force, then they have no choice but to listen to you.

"Don't worry, I will." Shadow and I look at each other, understanding exactly what we both mean.

"That's good," Shadow says this, but it doesn't really sound like she means it. "I really am sorry about what happened to your drawing earlier. It was very cruel of that boy, Alex, to do that to you just because you wouldn't let him copy your homework. You did the right thing by not letting him do that though. It wouldn't have been fair since he would get the same grade without having to do any work."

I have to hide a smile at her words. She sounds like a mom right now. The smile immediately disappears when I realize something. She has kind of become like a mother to me. Shadow is the one I talk to whenever I feel lost, she's the one who comforts me whenever someone picks on me at school, and she is the one who is always trying to push me to be a better person, always telling me that I am better than I think I am. I think she thinks too much of me sometimes. She keeps telling me that I am a talented, intelligent, and that people should be seen as lucky to be considered my friend. I honestly think the opposite. I'm kind of a pathetic moron, why else would everyone pick on me for my entire life? I want to improve myself, but I think it will take a while to do that.

I hang my head, feeling embarrassed that she is bringing that incident up again. I would rather just forget about what happened with Alex for now.

"It's okay. Like I said before, he's done worse to me. Thankfully I was able to finish another drawing for class pretty quick." I try to make it sound like I am not upset by this, but I can see by Shadow's gaze that she doesn't believe it but decides to ignore my little lie.

"I see, I am glad. I am surprised that the two of you used to be friends." She is right, we had been friends when we were in Kindergarten, but that changed as soon as everyone decided to start picking on me. After that he turned on me and never was my friend again. Sometimes I find myself missing those days, before all of my trouble started, but I can never go back. No matter how much I wish to be able to turn back time, life just doesn't work that way. If one of my superpowers could have been to go back in time, I think I would be a lot happier than I am now.

"Yeah, sometimes that seems like a dream instead of a memory, but someday soon we won't have to worry about him. Soon, his torture will only be a memory too. I will make sure of that." Shadow nods, her happiness fading.

"I'm guessing you have found someone to be your next soldier then?" I look down at her, suddenly feeling a bit awkward.

"No… no I haven't yet, but I will. I have a feeling that I will find the perfect person soon, don't you worry about that. I won't fail this time."

Shadows nods her head silently while I turn away from her to stare out my window to look out at Main Street. I wanted to turn away so that I wouldn't have to see that look on her feathered face. She didn't look as if she was worried that I won't find the perfect soldier, she looked as if she was afraid that I will.

People pass by on the street below me, going to their homes or running errands. I watch them all, but none of them see me. Truthfully that is how I always feel. I feel as if I am invisible, watching everyone as they go through their lives while none of them notice me. That is until they want to find someone that they can pick on, someone they can make fun of. I am only visible when they have a purpose for me. I have had that happen so many times that I won't even bother to try and count them.

I remember one time in particular that always depresses me whenever I think about it. I was in middle school and I was invisible then just like how I'm invisible now. One day, only a few days before a big school dance, one of the prettiest girls in the school, and my crush at the time, asked if I could take her to the dance. I should have seen what they were planning, it seems so obvious to me now. I had bought the tickets to the dance for the both of us as well as some nice clothes to wear and did everything I could to make myself look good for her. I didn't want such a pretty girl to look bad by being with an unattractive guy like me. I even went and got her some flowers because I thought she was as interested in me as I was in her. She told me that I didn't need to pick her up, she would meet me at the school. I should have seen that as a sign for what was going to happen.

I walked into the school gym with the biggest smile on my face. I felt like the luckiest guy in the world. I felt that way until I could finally see the reality that had been staring at me in the face. Standing in line to give their tickets to one of our teachers was the girl I had thought had been my date hanging onto the arm of Alex. She was laughing hard at something he had said while he held her close. It felt as if the world had disappeared beneath me and I was falling forever. I should have run away at that point when I figured out what had happened, but I couldn't move. I was so shocked that I just stayed there and stared at the two of them. Alex noticed me after about a minute that felt like hours to me. He left his date to walk over to me with the biggest smile on his arrogant face. When he stood in front of me, he laughed in my face.

"Did you really think that a girl like her would ever go out with an ugly little creep like you?" Other people could overhear what Alex was saying to me and stopped to listen, smiling in amusement at my pain. "I would have thought that you had more sense than that Louie. I hope you have a fun night dancing by yourself." He walked away from me to return to his date while all of the people who had been listening in started laughing at me. All of them surrounded me in a circle of humiliation as their laughter just seemed to grow louder and louder.

When I looked at the girl that I had cared for laughing at me along with everyone else, I finally saw her as she truly was. She was just a mean girl like all of the others in my school. At that moment, for the first time in my life, I wished that I had remained invisible. Everyone was staring at me then, laughing at me as if I was something less than human. They could all see me, but nobody helped me. Nobody wanted to help the pathetic loser of the school.

I ran out of the gym that night, not even bothering to go to the dance. I called my uncle to pick me up, but I had to wait around twenty minutes in the dark night before he was able to come. That night I looked up at the night sky and felt more alone than I had ever felt before. I wished that I could just disappear in the sky with the stars where nobody else could find me and hurt me. When my Uncle Diego was finally able to pick me up, he tried to ask me what had happened and why I wasn't at the dance with my date. I just told him that I didn't want to talk about it. We spent the rest of the car ride home in silence. I never did tell him about what happened that night, but I think he has probably figured it out by now.

I force the memory of that awful night out of my mind, not wanting to feel depressed over something that happened years ago. There is enough depressing stuff happening right now that can keep me miserable, I don't need to think of stuff from the past to make it any worse.

As I continue to look down on the street below my room an endless stream of people pass by on the sidewalk. I feel anger rising in me as I watch them. I want someone to look up and see me. I don't want to feel so invisible anymore. I don't want to be alone. I smile when I think about how I have been shown on the news as the Crow whenever I have fought against Silver Dove. Those are the only times when it feels as if I am being seen, as if I can be heard. My smile grows wider as I think something directed to the people beneath me. Just wait, you will all see me again soon, and you will all pay attention to me.

Chapter Five

Colomba-
My Father
Notices

Walking into my house, I greet my grandmother who is cooking dinner on the stove. From what I can see, it looks as if she is cooking pasta with pesto. Walking into the living room, my dad is sitting in his favorite armchair, reading a book. He looks over his book when he notices that he isn't alone in the room anymore.

"Hello Sweetheart, how are you today?" Dad says as he puts down his book with a smile on his face, giving me his full attention.

"I'm alright I guess. Not much really happened today so I can't complain. Just a normal day." My father looks at me with a careful, examining eye and I can tell that he can see through my little lie.

"Colomba can you come over here for a

minute?" I walk over to him and sit on the arm of his chair. He looks me in the eyes, worry in his gaze.

"Are you alright Colomba?" I blink a few times in surprise.

"Yeah, of course I'm alright. Why do you ask?" He looks away from me as he sets his book on a small table beside his chair and clears his throat like he always does whenever he has to say something that he is uncomfortable with.

"Well you've just been acting very oddly lately. You act as if you're worried about something, but you won't talk to me about it even though you used to be able to tell me everything. You don't look very well either. You look as if you haven't slept in weeks. Please tell me what's wrong." I lower my head feeling a bit ashamed for lying to my father.

I did used to tell my father everything, but lately I have been keeping a lot of secrets from him. I haven't told my father that I am Silver Dove. I haven't told him that I fought against the Crow twice. And I haven't told him that Grandma is the one who gave me these powers in the form of a magical pin that I always wear now. I have barely told him anything. Grandma warned me that if I told my dad about what I have been up to as Silver Dove then he might try to stop me. He would want me to be safe and fighting against monsters isn't very safe now is it? I can't risk that, so I have to keep this major secret from someone I love. It really hurts having to lie to him, but I know that I have to if I am going to do my job as Silver Dove.

"Is it because of the Crow?" I feel my eyes grow wide as I look back up at him. What does he mean by that? Does he know more than I have told him? Does he know who I really am?

"What are you talking about Dad?"

"Well I think everyone has been a bit on edge ever since he first showed up at your school. I wouldn't be surprised if he has bothered you too with everything he has been doing. You have always been a very sensitive girl, having something terrible like this happen at your own school must be very distressing for you." I instantly calm down, feeling safe again.

"Yeah it was pretty scary. I've been having some nightmares about it. I'm just afraid that he will come back and I won't know what to do." He takes my small hand in his, practically covering it with his much larger hand.

"You will just need to hide in a safe place with some of your friends and let Silver Dove handle it. She will know what to do. She will keep everyone safe. She has to." I look down, not wanting to look him in the eyes.

"Yes, I suppose she does have to." My father notices my discomfort, but he doesn't realize my true reason.

"Don't worry Dear. I'm sure that Silver Dove will solve everything, and the Crow will go away some time soon. You'll see. Everything will be alright again someday and none of us will have to worry about this again. You just stay strong a little bit longer and things will get better." I still don't look at him when I give him my reply.

"I hope so too Dad. I really hope so." I give him a quick kiss before heading up to my room. When I get there, I look in the mirror above my dresser to see what my dad had meant when he said that I didn't look very well. Looking at my reflection I can **easily** see what he meant. Dark circles haunt underneath my eyes and my face looks drawn. My eyes also lack any kind of life, they are dull. I look like a zombie. I really do need to get some sleep, but no matter how hard I try I just can't seem to close my eyes without having nightmares. I turn my face away from my reflection, feeling ashamed. Why am I so afraid? I have superpowers too. I have fought the Crow twice and he has disappeared both times. Shouldn't I feel proud instead of terrified? Why am I so afraid of someone I have already beaten multiple times?

Maybe it's because I don't know when he will be coming back or what he will do. I know that he's not giving up on his weird mission. He's too determined to quit already. If that guy has quit, then

I'm a unicorn. I guess the waiting for him to come back is the worst part. Since I don't know what will happen when he does, I don't know what to expect. Not knowing is something that has always bothered me. I always need to know what to expect or else I get nervous. Thanks to the Crow I never know what to expect.

The Crow is going to drive me crazy one of these days I just know it. At least that is something I can expect. I take another quick glance at myself in the mirror and see my tired eyes and I can't help but think that he may have already started on making me crazy. What other word would describe how I am right now? I am a nervous wreck, I have barely slept because of some nightmares, and I have a hard time just doing the usual things of the day because I am so tired.

I lay down on top of my bed, not even bothering to get under the covers. Hopefully I can have a bit of time to sleep before Grandma is done making dinner. Hopefully I can have a bit of peace, even if it's just for a few minutes.

Chapter Six

Luis-
Trying

Placing my finished homework back into my
backpack on top of my desk, I walk over to my
window and glance down at the people walking on
Main Street beneath me. I think about what Shadow
and I had talked about earlier. I had openly told her
that I don't know who my next soldier will be, and I
was being perfectly honest. I really have no idea. I
have made a list of all the bullied kids in the school
that I know about, yet I still can't find the right one.
It is a very long list, but I don't see one person on it
that would be worthy of getting superpowers from
me. No matter who I look at on that list, they just
aren't right. I always find something wrong with
them, so I decide not to choose them. It's really
frustrating me.

More than anything I want to just have my next

soldier succeed so that I can stop this and have everybody stop picking on each other all the time. I was on A- Streamer, a popular social media website in my town, and I saw a bunch of mean posts calling a girl in my math class fat. I don't know that girl very well, but I do know that she is very nice. She wouldn't hurt a fly, yet nobody has a problem hurting her. Why are they hurting somebody who hasn't done a thing to them? It doesn't make any sense. Why don't people just make sense for once?

I draw the curtains to my room so that the fading light can't come in from the setting sun. It is now darker in my room, but I like it that way. Ever since I have become the Crow, I have found the darkness far more inviting. Heading over to my desk, I pull out my sketchbook and flip to the first empty page I can find. I stare at the blank page with my pencil above it, trying to figure out what I can draw. In this sketchbook, I have very few pages drawn on. The only other thing in here is my sketch of a crow and Tigerclaw. I want to use this sketchbook to record all of the stuff I've done as the Crow, so I plan on putting all of my soldiers in this book so that I can always remember them. I smile when I realize something obvious. This is my sketchbook for myself as the Crow, but I haven't drawn the Crow yet. Kind of a stupid mistake.

I immediately get to work, imagining how I look when I am the Crow. I start on my face and move outward. As I work on the feathers of my wings, I make large angry strokes with my pencil as I think about all of the things people have said about me as the Crow. They don't know what they're talking about. I smile as I move away from the drawing of myself as the Crow and begin to draw other people around me, my loyal followers. I sketch the faces of other kids that I know are getting picked on in school, the ones I know who would support me and what I am doing. My heart seems to grow inside of me when I watch their faces being created by my pencil. They all seem to understand that I am trying to do the right thing. I am trying to make the world a better place in the only way that people understand, force.

Behind myself in the drawing, I sketch out Silver Dove. This is what I am trying to do. I want Silver Dove to stand behind me. We are meant to work together. She should understand that I am the right one and she should follow me too. One day she will get some sense and join my side so that we can make this world a better place. One day that I don't think will happen any time soon. She keeps saying that I am the bad guy. She couldn't be more wrong. Silver Dove is the bad guy, not me. Why can't everybody else see that too?

I set my pencil down to examine my almost finished drawing. It does look very nice with my followers standing beside me, encouraging me in my fight, but I have left one spot blank. The spot right beside me. My smile quickly disappears when I look at it. I know who I want to put there, but I don't know if they will ever join me. I want to draw Colomba there, but she has never said anything even remotely good about the Crow. Most of what she has said about me has been cold and hurtful. I know that she doesn't mean to be. There isn't a mean bone in her body, but she doesn't know that I am the Crow, so she says these things to my face without knowing how much it hurts me to hear it. I can never tell her how much her words have hurt me. I don't think I can even come up with the words to explain how much pain it causes me.

I close my sketchbook, not wanting to look at that sketch anymore. Placing the sketchbook back in my desk drawer, I close the drawer with a slam. Why can't they all just see that I am trying to do the right thing? I am trying to make the pain end. I am trying to make myself truly happy for the first time in my life.

I am trying.

Chapter Seven

Colomba-
My Fear

Sitting in my room, I finish up an assignment for my math class before I put it back in my backpack and lay down on my bed, closing my eyes. Even though it is only a little after six o'clock, and I took a small nap before dinner, I already feel like going to bed. Last night I probably only got around three hours of sleep and I definitely feel it now. I feel like I am moving in slow motion. The world is moving so quickly, but I am stuck moving at a snail's pace.

Opening my eyes, I look up at my ceiling, completely lost in my thoughts. My mind wanders back to a dark thought I had after I had defeated the Crow when he had Tigerclaw attack the school. I have no control over my life anymore. Grandma had pointed out to me that I will have to keep going against the Crow for as long as he still thinks this negative way. Thinking that he has to do all of these bad things to help the people in our school. If he never gives up on this idea, then I will have to stay here forever so that I can keep stopping him. I will never be able to go away to college, I can't be a doctor like I've always wanted, and I can't really do anything with my life except continually stopping the Crow from doing stupid stuff.

What can I do with my life if I keep having to try and stop the Crow? Will I just have to get a boring job that I don't want to do so that I can survive while taking on the Crow every spare minute? I don't want to live that way. I want to become a doctor and have a family. None of that involves the Crow. I don't want to do this for the rest of my life! I want to have a life! I can't have a life if the Crow is in it!

I have to convince him that he is doing the wrong thing, or he needs to figure it out on his own. One day, one of us is going to give up. I don't think that me or the Crow want to keep having an endless struggle between us. Either one of us gives up, or one of us is defeated. I can only hope that we both give up, or the Crow gets defeated. I can only imagine what things would be like if the Crow defeated me. As I let myself travel deeper into my thoughts, I imagine what it would really be like if the Crow won.

If the Crow defeated me, he wouldn't just be

satisfied with ending the bullying in my school. He would make sure that every person who he thought of as a bully would suffer. Someone as evil as him would probably take over this town and force every bully in town to be his slave. Letting everyone else live in his town with him ruling over them like a king, everyone living in fear of him. I shudder when I think about what he would do to me. If he found out my true identity, he would probably kill me and then give my Dove Pin to one of his loyal followers who would use my powers to do whatever the Crow wanted of them. If he won, all hope would be lost. I bury my face in my hands as my heart sinks into my chest. I have no choice. I have to keep fighting him no matter what, even if I have to sacrifice my own happiness. I will do it to keep everyone safe and happy.

Picking myself off my bed, I walk over to my window and open it up, letting the night air blow on my face. I close my eyes in peace as I breathe in the scent of flowers coming from my grandmother's garden in the backyard. I need to fly, that's what I need. That will definitely help me feel better. Without giving it a second thought, I place my hand over my pin, say the magic words, and I am almost instantly transformed into Silver Dove. I smile weakly at the sight of my beautiful wings before I leap out of my bedroom window and take off into the darkening sky where only a few stars are able to be seen.

I fly high, higher than usual. With my heart falling I want to go higher. I want to feel alive since I feel so empty inside. I soar through the clouds, I feel the water from the clouds sticking to the feathers of my wings, but I don't care. I usually hate the feeling of having wet feathers, but at the moment I couldn't care less.

As I fly as high as I can, I reach my hand up toward the brightest star in the sky. It almost feels as if I can touch it, but I know I can't. As I look at that star, my heart feels like it is breaking. I can never reach it, just like the dreams I have made for myself. As my world gets darker and darker, I feel as if I am being covered by the wings of the Crow. I feel a tear falling beneath my mask as I turn my face away from that star, not wanting to look at it anymore. I close my wings and my eyes, feeling my body fall through the air. The wind rushes around me for a moment before I open my eyes again to stare at the ground beneath me that is quickly getting closer and closer. When the small shapes on the ground begin to take form into buildings and farmland, I open my wings again, catching myself as I soar through the sky, heading back home.

Flying over the farmland, cows look up at me as they graze in the pasture. I am glad that there aren't any people out tonight since I would rather not be seen. I don't want word getting around to my grandma that I had been flying around in the middle of the night. Grandma is usually really nice, but if you have done something wrong then you will see a darker side of her that you would never expect to see. I know that I would see that side if she found out that I had gone out flying in the middle of the night without her permission.

I fly back into my window and transform back into my normal self before I let myself curl up under my covers. My head hits the pillow, but I still can't sleep despite how tired I am. As I stare up at my dark ceiling, I can only think one thing that keeps repeating over and over again. I am lost.

Chapter Eight

Luis-
For My Own
Protection

The bus pulls in front of the school and Nat, Colomba, and I hop off to head inside. Colomba and Nat leave me as they run ahead to try and catch up to someone they share a class with to talk about an assignment, leaving me all alone. At first, this doesn't bother me, that is until I see that someone else has noticed that I am alone, Alex.

I feel my body stiffen in fear at the sight of the anger in his eyes. I know why he is angry. He wanted to get me alone after school yesterday so he could beat me up for not letting him copy my homework, which made him get in trouble for not completing it. I had hoped and prayed that he would have forgotten about that by now, but from the fire in his eyes as he looks at me, I guess he hasn't. I should have known that hoping he would forget would be a stupid idea. I should never have hope when it comes to him. He practically marches through the crowd heading to the front doors to get to me while I hurry to try and make it through those doors, knowing that I will be safer in there. Even though I am going as fast as I can through that crowd Alex is just getting closer to me. He actually pushes a few people out of the way so that he can get to me. He will make it to me before I can get inside. Who knows what he will do to me if he does catch me?

I notice a hole in the crowd in front of me. I try harder to get through so I can make it to that hole, if I do then I can move faster in the crowd. When I do make it to the hole, I instantly understand why everyone had created that hole. They were avoiding a large puddle of mud on the ground that must have formed from the small rain shower we had really early this morning. Glancing back, I can see that Alex is only a few feet away from me and is closing the distance too quickly for me to be able to get away. In my panic, I do something that I wouldn't have dared to do if I wasn't so terrified.

At the last minute, when Alex almost has his hands on me, I lunge out of the way, but keep my foot in the same spot. With his speed, and my foot in the way, Alex doesn't have a chance to stop or slow down before he trips over my foot and lands face first in the giant puddle of mud with a huge splash. The entire world seems to stand still. Everyone has turned to look at what has just happened while my heart pounds in my chest. All of them are silent in their shock as Alex picks himself up from the puddle. His entire front is covered in mud, his clothes are soaked, and a thick layer of the brown liquid now covers his face and drips from his hair. When I look at his mud-covered face as he wipes it out of his eyes I do one of the stupidest things I have ever done. I laugh, I laugh my heart out. This breaks the silence and the entire school joins me in the laughter. Laughing at the guy who has been picking on practically every person in this place. Laughing at the real monster at this school. I have to admit that this is probably one of the most beautiful things I have ever seen in my entire life. I know that is mean to say, but it feels nice to be able to laugh at the person who has hurt me too many times to count over the years we have known each other.

Even though I am looking at the funniest thing I have ever seen I know I can't enjoy it for long. While the crowd is standing still, laughing at Alex, I make my way past them and make it through the front doors before Alex can catch me. If I had stayed a minute longer, Alex would have grabbed me and beaten me to a pulp and then thrown me in the puddle too so I would be just as dirty as him. From the way he glared at me as I laughed at him, I wouldn't be surprised if he would have tried to drown me in that puddle if he had caught me. I am still chuckling when I make it to my first class. The first bell rings, starting class, but Alex is still not here even though this is one of the classes that we share. He's probably in the bathroom right now trying to get the mud off.

I chuckle softly to myself at that thought but it is quickly cut short when I realize the obvious. I'm going to die now. Alex is going to kill me. I am only fourteen, but I am going to die. I may have only done that for my own protection, I didn't even plan on doing it, it just happened but that doesn't matter. No matter what though, Alex is going to kill me.

Chapter Nine

Colomba-
Terrible
News

The first bell rings and everyone piles through the front doors of the school to head to their first class. I am in the center of the mass of people. Since I am smaller than most, I get bumped around a bit most of the time, but this doesn't bother me. The people around me don't mean to do it. Everyone is so tightly packed together that it is almost impossible not to bump into the people next to you. When you are around so many people it is also impossible not to overhear some peoples' conversations.

"Did you hear about her car accident? I heard it was really bad, only she got hurt though." I try to look and see who was talking about this, but I can't find the person in the massive group around me. From somewhere else, I hear another voice that seems to be talking about the same thing.

"I can't believe the rotten luck, to be hurt now, of all times. I guess that we can only hope that what we've been hearing isn't true. This is going to mean trouble, anybody with eyes can see that." Well I must have lost my eyes without knowing because I have no idea what's going on. What on earth are they talking about? What car accident? Who was hurt? What trouble is going to happen because of it? I am so confused.

My first few classes go by quickly, but I don't find answers to these questions until I walk into my gym class. Everything looks normal, except for the fact that Cheyanne is still missing. Everyone is gathered in the center of the gym, talking amongst themselves while we wait for the coach to start class. Just like what usually happens, I am greeted by Alex as soon as I have joined the group.

"Hey Beautiful, have you heard the news?" I look into his eyes, he's obviously eager to tell me about the "news" he is referring to. I can see that there are still little bits of dirt stuck in his hair from when he fell in that mud puddle earlier today. I have heard a lot of people talking about it, but I decide not to ask him about it. He probably still feels pretty embarrassed even though he has cleaned himself up already. Most of the people who talked about it were pretty happy when they were retelling the story, as if they were happy that Alex was embarrassed by all of this. I can understand why they were happy. I have heard a lot of people talk about mean things that Alex has done, but it still seems a bit cruel to laugh at his pain.

"No, what's up?" He wraps his arm around my shoulder before I have a chance to react. His confidence always shocks me somehow.

"Cheyanne was in a car accident yesterday. That's why she isn't at school." I quickly move out of his grip to face him, fear making my eyes grow wide.

"You're kidding!" My heart is pounding while my muscles feel tense. "Is she alright? Was anybody hurt?" Alex shrugs his shoulders at me, a smile on his face, knowing that he has my full attention.

"Nobody else got hurt. Apparently she was driving to school yesterday and swerved her car to avoid hitting a dog and hit a tree instead. I think she is the only one who got hurt. I don't know how badly she's hurt, but I know she was in the hospital all day yesterday." I close my eyes and turn away from Alex, not wanting to let him see the pain I feel inside. Poor Cheyanne, I can only hope that everything is alright with her. I can only hope that she isn't in any pain.

When the coach comes in and starts class, he says that we can either play basketball or jump rope. The coach looks a bit depressed so I'm guessing he has already heard about what happened to his track star. As I start jumping rope, Alex tries to talk to me about what he is doing in practice and how he thinks that everyone else on his teams are terrible except him. He says that the only way that his teams even have a chance of winning is if they let him play throughout each of the games. Just like how I usually handle this when Alex starts showing off, I let my mind wander into my own thoughts. I ignore him for the most part.

I can only hope that Cheyanne is alright. I'm not sure if we would be considered friends since we don't talk very much, but she is very kind and I wouldn't want anything bad to happen to her. Even though she is very popular because she is a star on the track team, she is kind to everyone and doesn't let her popularity go to her head. It wouldn't be fair to have someone as kind as her to be hurt like that, so soon before the biggest sporting event of her life.

While Alex goes on and on about his athletic achievements I think about Cheyanne. I am hoping and praying that Alex is wrong, that Cheyanne will be alright and that everything goes back to normal. Or at least as normal as our school can get. Not much that has happened since I started at this school that can be considered normal. I suppose that many people would consider that a good thing. Most people would probably like having a not normal life since that would be more exciting, but more than anything I just want a normal life right now. I want to be able to go to school without feeling afraid about what the Crow might do. I want to talk to my friends without having the huge secret about me being Silver Dove hanging over my head. And I want to be able to go to bed and have a peaceful night's sleep. I think I want that last one more than anything. I just want to not be afraid all the time. Is that too much to ask for?

Chapter Ten

Luis-
A Fallen
Hero

Yesterday at lunch Colomba told me all about how that girl from the track team, Cheyanne, got into a car accident. She seemed so worried about her even though they aren't really that good of friends. Sometimes I am amazed at how much she cares about everyone. It's as if she cares more about others than herself. She really is an angel.

Now that a new day has started, I wait and see if I can see this girl that Colomba was telling me about. I've never really talked to Cheyanne before, but it would be practically impossible for anyone in this school to not know what she looks like. She has been on the front page of our school newspaper so often that everyone at this school has her face memorized. When I walk through the hallways, my eyes scan through the crowd, trying to find her. I look from face to face, but I don't see hers until right after my second period has ended and I am heading to my third.

Standing at one end of the hallway, I look through the crowd and see her easily. Everyone is keeping their distance from her, as if she has some kind of terrible disease. When I look at her, I understand why they don't want to be close. People are openly insulting her as she passes them, throwing things at the back of her head as she tries to peacefully make it to her next class. Her books are in a large bag that swings from side to side as she slowly moves down the hall. I bet that she wishes more than anything that she could move faster but in her condition I don't think that is possible.

Despite the fact that she is being harassed and bullied in plain sight, nobody does anything to stop it, not even the teachers. They just pass by, pretending that they don't see a thing. Some of the other students look at her with pity, but none of them help her, none of them even try to help. I want to scream at them for being so cruel, but I know that would only get me in trouble. Sometimes you get in trouble even if you are trying to do the right thing. That's just how the world works I guess.

While I watch her, someone throws a bottle of water at her, hitting her in the back. She stumbles a little at the impact, but then keeps moving as if nothing happened. I know that she knew what happened though since I see tears beginning to form in her eyes. One falls down her face, but she quickly wipes it away with the back of her hand, trying to hide the fact that she is crying form everyone else. When she passes by me I hear her sniffling softly while her eyes are starting to grow red from her tears. She holds back sobs that threaten to escape her lips, but I can still notice them. I have had to hold back many tears in my life because of my bullies. I know how to recognize it in other people too. It is always a sad sight to see, seeing someone else sharing the same pain that you go through all the time, especially someone who has never experienced it before like Cheyanne. At least I am used to getting picked on all the time. I know how it works, but she is completely unfamiliar with it. She doesn't know what to do and I don't think she would ever want to hear my advice on how to be the newest school outcast. It is hard to admit, especially to yourself, that you are no longer welcome someplace just because of who you are. I had to admit that to myself a long time ago, and I have had to keep reminding myself about it over the years. It doesn't get any easier, it just stays the same level of awful as it always does.

As I watch her miserably move down the hallway, I feel a smile forming on my face. I believe that a plan is beginning to form around this girl. My smile grows wider as I hear another person throw an insult at Cheyanne as she turns down another hallway to probably receive the same treatment she got down this hallway. I run through the hall until I reach the boy's bathroom. Making sure that nobody else is in there, I place my hand over my medal and Shadow appears almost instantly.

"You saw what I saw didn't you?" Shadow nods her head, her eyes closed in her sadness.

"Yes I did. I feel so terribly sad for that poor girl. To be hurt like that and be ridiculed for it is unforgivable." I chuckle at her words, my happiness growing inside of me.

"I know what you mean, but I know how we can help. She is absolutely perfect. I mean what can be sadder than a fallen hero?"

Chapter Eleven

Colomba-Cheyanne

Between each class, I search for Cheyanne. I heard that she's back in school today, but for some reason everyone isn't happy about it. Shouldn't they be excited that she's well enough to be back in school after what happened? Why isn't everyone glad that she's back? I haven't really heard anything else except that she is back. Kinda strange considering she was the only thing people could talk about yesterday. It's almost like everyone is avoiding talking about her. I just don't understand what's going on. I finally get my answers when I am walking through the halls after my second class of the day.

As I pass through the hallway, a familiar face stands out to me in the crowd. She is just making her way into this hallway. There is a wide space around her, really strange considering that everyone is usually packed together in the halls because there are so many people here. I lift my hand to wave at Cheyanne, but something stops me, something that sends a stone down to my stomach and my mouth hangs open in shock and despair. Cheyanne is a very tall girl with wavy hair that is somewhere between blonde and brunette. Her usually happy brown eyes are now cast down in misery, and I know why. Wrapped around one of her legs is a large, pink cast. I lower my hand quickly, feeling suddenly uncomfortable. With her leg broken she won't be able to run in nationals this year. Without her the team probably won't win like they had been expecting.

Looking at the people around her, many of them glare down at Cheyanne as she hobbles down the hallway on her crutches. Even without them saying anything I know what they are thinking. They think she has let everyone down because of her injury. The entire school had been so excited about one of our teams going to nationals and now that dream is shattered. In their eyes she is a traitor for getting hurt and ruining the team's chances of victory, but in Cheyanne's eyes all I see is misery and disappointment. A few people look at her with pity, but nobody steps forward to talk to her, to make her feel better. I think that they are too afraid of the other people around her who are glaring at her. Afraid that they might be made fun of too if they help her.

Running up to her, she tries to give me a smile as I start walking beside her but it is faint and barely even noticeable.

"Hey Cheyanne, I heard about your accident. I am so sorry that this happened." Cheyanne chuckles without any humor.

"I guess you're the only one. You're the first one to say that to me all morning. Everybody else is ignoring me or saying that I suck for letting this happen."

"But it's not like you wanted this to happen. Why are they blaming you for something that was an accident?" She shrugs at me.

"I guess they just want someone to blame for the school not winning at nationals." I look in her eyes that are cast down at the ground as she tries to move with her crutches and I walk slowly so that she can keep up with me.

"Do you want to talk about it?" Cheyanne stops for a moment, her eyes tightly closed. I have the sudden feeling that she is about to cry but she merely shakes her head and keeps hobbling on her crutches. I can see that she is holding back the tears, trying to be strong in a very difficult situation.

"I don't know Colomba. I feel like I want to talk but I know it won't do any good. It won't change anything. It won't change how everyone is treating me and it won't fix my leg!"

"It may not change how everyone else treats you or your leg, but it may make you feel better about it if you get it off your chest." Cheyanne stops again to face me, glaring at me coldly.

"Well what do you want me to tell you Colomba? Do you want me to tell you how people keep treating me like they saw me beat up a puppy? It's not my fault that I broke my leg in that car crash! I wanted to run in nationals! I wanted it more than anything! Now I can't do that *and* my friends all ditched me! I don't know what to do." I am about to say something when she starts walking again as quickly as she can with her leg in a cast. "Whatever, nobody wants to listen to me whine about this. I'll see you later Colomba." She hobbles away on her crutches while I try to follow her through the massive crowd of people, but I get farther and farther behind her. I try to call her back to me. I want to talk to her more so that she won't feel so alone, but she keeps hobbling away, not even bothering to look back at me. When she is no longer in sight I give up trying to catch up to her. Hanging my head, I walk to my next class feeling as if I have failed a friend in their time of need.

Chapter Twelve

Luis-
A New Plan

Keeping my eyes glued to Cheyanne, I watch her misery with a smile on my face. Her lunch period started only a few minutes ago, but Cheyanne isn't eating in the cafeteria with everyone else. She is eating standing up in the hallway. I can only imagine how uncomfortable it must be with that massive cast on her leg. It's obvious why she is staying as far away from the cafeteria as possible, the less people she is around the less likely people will harass her.

I have been keeping my eye on her all day and listening in on people talking about her. Everyone hates her now just because she got hurt and can't win nationals for the school. Everyone thinks she is the worst person on the face of the earth when they were praising her just the other day. Are sports really this important to people? I don't get it, but I've always been more of a bookish, artsy guy. Sports aren't really my thing. Never have been and probably never will be. I fall on my face nearly every time I try to do anything athletic.

As I watch her try to enjoy her sandwich in peace, another member of the track team walks up to Cheyanne with her arms crossed in front of her chest. Cheyanne, when she first notices this girl, smiles at her, but that smile quickly fades when she sees that the girl doesn't return her smile. Cheyanne had probably thought of this girl as a friend before she got hurt. Obviously the girl doesn't consider her to be a friend anymore. The girl glares at her for a moment, looking at her cast covered leg with particular disgust before she speaks.

"You should have just stayed away from school. Nobody wants you here." Cheyanne glares at the person she had thought of as a friend. She glares at them with the eyes of someone who has been betrayed, the eyes of someone who has lost hope.

"I was hoping that I would come back to find that I had friends who wanted to comfort me and stand by my side. I guess that I was wrong." Cheyanne's ex-friend walks away in a huff, her nose in the air as if she is so much better than the girl she is leaving behind. The warning bell rings and I leave quickly to head to my next class.

Only after a few minutes into the class, I ask the teacher if I can go to the bathroom. When I am alone in the hallway I chuckle to myself as I think about what I had just seen with Cheyanne and that other girl. Maybe she is the one I have been searching for. Just the other day she was at the top in this school and now she is being crushed at the bottom. Even though I have always been at the bottom, I can still feel pity toward this girl, knowing that she is a kind person who doesn't deserve this. My smile grows wider when I think about my plans for her. She may be the perfect one to be my next soldier. She has something that Tigerclaw didn't have. She is stronger. Tigerclaw may have wanted her revenge, but this girl already has the determination and skill of an athlete. She won't back down just because Silver Dove talks to her, she will be determined to reach her goal and will stop at nothing to get it. Tigerclaw was weak to begin with, but this girl has something more than just the desire for revenge. She has been betrayed by the people who had been her friends. That can make a person do anything, even join sides with me.

As soon as I am alone in the bathroom, I place my hand over my medal so that Shadow can appear. She shakes her dark feathers as she perches herself on a paper towel dispenser.

"Hello Master, what can I do for you?" I smile at her, feeling the anticipation building inside me, knowing that my plan is finally starting again.

"I'm sure you saw what happened back there. It's time to help her get back the respect she deserves." Shadow nods her head solemnly, knowing exactly what I mean by that comment. "Transform me into the Crow. It's time." I close my eyes as Shadow begins to fly rapidly around me and I open my eyes soon after to see that Shadow is gone and I am now in the costume of the Crow. Smiling, I whisper, "Shadow find Cheyanne."

I feel Shadow leaving me even though I can't see her. I close my eyes so that I can see what she sees. I watch as I let Shadow leave me to fly through the halls until she finally reaches the person who is standing by themselves, trying to calmly eat their lunch without bringing any attention to themselves. Shadow flies straight into her heart. I can already feel the misery there even though I haven't completely taken her over yet.

Hello Cheyanne. Cheyanne tries to turn around quickly but can't because of her injury. Instead she just has to look around rapidly, trying to find where the mysterious voice is coming from. I can feel her heart pounding in her chest in her terror. I have to control myself to keep from laughing.

I am the Crow, I want to help you. I can make you the fastest runner on the team again. I can make them all regret hurting you. I can make sure that they never doubt you again. She looks nervous about what I am saying, but also very excited.

"W- what do you want me to do?" I smile, knowing that I have her in my grasp.

Just join me and I can make sure that you get everything you deserve. She and I now share a smile.

"I will do anything you want me to do." I chuckle softly to myself. Good, good, absolutely perfect. Shadow takes over her heart, where I feel all of the pain and betrayal she has felt since her accident. Shadow continues to take her over until only her mind is left, but there is no resistance there. Cheyanne is completely willing to let me in, to let me control her. As I feel her changing, the cast on her leg disappears and her broken bone quickly mends itself, letting her return back to her normal state, but I don't stop there. I know what she needs to become, she needs to go far beyond what she was before, better than what any human alive has had before. I know how to help her. I know what she needs to be. I smile as I let this girl become who she is meant to be.

Chapter Thirteen

Colomba-
Cheyanne
Forgotten

I am in my fourth period now, but my mind is miles away. I can't stop thinking about what happened in gym. The coach didn't talk about the track team at all, even though he couldn't stop talking about them a few days ago. Nationals is only a week or two away, yet he wouldn't talk about them. All he could talk about was the football and basketball team, something that Alex seemed to be happy about. Everyone seems to be trying to avoid the topic of Cheyanne and her injury. It's almost like she has died and nobody wants to talk about her because it would be too upsetting. This is all really weird. I don't understand any of this.

Everyone else may have been pretty silent during gym, but Alex surely wasn't. All through the class he wouldn't stop talking about the sports teams he's on, some stories that involved him doing some pretty impressive things, as well as his plans for the weekend. He seemed pretty eager to invite me to join him this weekend to see a movie, but I declined. I have a funny feeling that he would try to talk through the movie too since he talks through practically everything else. Sometimes it's as painful as getting your teeth pulled trying to talk to him since he always manages to bring the conversation back around to himself. It's almost impressive the way he can do that no matter what you're talking about. If I wasn't the one who had to listen to the conversation, I would find it kind of funny.

At the moment, I am finishing up an assignment as my eyes begin to cloud over in my exhaustion. Just like every night since the Crow showed his ugly face at this school, I wasn't able to sleep much last night. If I keep going like this, I'm going to fall asleep while crossing the street and get run over or something. That would be a very sad way to go. The Crow is destroying me, and he hasn't even showed up again in a while. The Crow really does control my life. I close my eyes as a pain seems to flow through my body at that thought. I am just a puppet in his hands. How on earth can I protect my school if I can't even protect my own mind from the Crow's influence? What can I do as

Silver Dove if the Crow scares me so badly that I have nightmares that keep me up for over four months? I am so worthless. I'm more worthless than an ice- cream seller in the arctic.

When I look back down at the assignment in front of me, I can no longer focus on it. All I can think about is the Crow. The image of his masked face just keeps flashing through my mind. I see him sneering at me, enjoying the fact that I am miserable because of him. He is laughing at me because I am weak and he has power over me. I would punch him in his snarky little face if I could, but he is only in my head. I try to answer the last few questions on the worksheet while I hear the Crow's laugh echoing in the back of my mind. Only when I have answered the final question and turned in the worksheet do I rest my head on my desk and pray for sleep.

Sleep does come, but not restful sleep. As soon as my eyes have closed, I am being chased by a huge crowd of those demon dogs that the Crow has created. There are so many of those monsters that they seem to cover the earth. I can't even see the ground beneath the mass of dark shadow creatures that snarl and bark at me viciously. They all rush at me, trying to outrun each other, eager to be the one that takes me down. I can feel their hot breath on the back of my neck as they get closer and closer to me. The Crow watches all of this, laughing the entire time as his monsters pounce on me and dig their fangs into my armor. There are so many on top of me. I am being crushed. I can barely breathe under all of their weight. The Crow isn't concerned that I am being killed by his creations. He is enjoying the show. His laughter never stops. He barely even pauses to catch his breath. From him, all I can hear is an endless stream of that terrible, evil laugh. I yell out and scream in my terror with what little breath I have left, but the Crow doesn't show me any mercy. The Crow just keeps laughing at me, happy to know that he has finally defeated me.

The dogs rip apart my armor while the Crow steps forward and removes my helmet, revealing my face to him. He smiles even wider when he sees me, shaking his head in amusement.

"Oh Colomba, you should have known that you couldn't beat me. I have always been stronger than you. You knew that, so why did you keep trying to fight me? You should have just joined me when you had the chance, maybe then I would have forgiven you and you wouldn't have to be punished." He tosses my helmet aside and walks away as his dogs now begin to bite into me. I scream in agony, but the Crow doesn't help me, he doesn't even turn around. He walks away, leaving me to my misery, to my "punishment". As one of the dogs bites into my throat, I feel myself jolt awake.

I glance around the room to see that nothing unusual has happened. I am still safe. Even though I repeat to myself that I am safe my heart still pounds in my chest, as if I really had been running away from those demon dogs. As if I had been attacked. I rub my throat where the demon dog in my dream had bitten me. In the back of my mind I can still feel the pain from its teeth and I can still hear that terrible laugh echoing in my skull. My hands tremble on my desk in my fear and my fury as the laugh just continues on and on, mocking me and my pain. I can still hear his voice when he told me that I should have joined his side, he is stronger than me, I shouldn't have kept fighting. As I try to stretch my stiff body in my chair I can feel the exhaustion in my muscles. I do know that he is stronger than me. How can I possibly beat him if he makes me so terrified even when he hasn't shown his face in a while? Why am I still trying to fight?

Chapter Fourteen

Luis-
My Second
Soldier

My newest soldier runs through the hallway to make it outside where the track team is meeting. The school has given them special permission to skip this period so that they can practice for nationals, and my soldier wants to see them more than anything. I want to see them too. I want to see the looks on their faces when they see the new Cheyanne.

They will definitely be surprised when they see her, she doesn't look like herself at all. She is wearing a tight-fitting outfit that covers her from head to toe, all in red and black. Dark, thick shades cover her eyes, making sure that nothing gets in her eyes when she is running at high speeds like this.

Even though she is running through a crowded

hallway, none of the people in the hall could ever catch her. Cheyanne, now my newest soldier, the Sprinter, can run faster than any person alive. She practically flies through the halls as her newly healed leg carries her to the other side of the school and out the back door in the matter of a few seconds. The Sprinter runs straight through the track field and then straight to the group of girls on the track team who had been standing close together discussing what they plan on doing at nationals without Cheyanne. She practically crashes through them, sending most of them falling to the ground in an angry heap. It only takes them a moment to stand up again with furious words, demanding that she tells them who she thinks she is. The Sprinter looks down at them proudly, a large grin spread across her face.

"Don't you recognize me? I'm the Sprinter, remember?" All of the girls' eyes grow wide as they recognize the nickname that they had given to their friend Cheyanne. The Sprinter smirks at them, chuckling softly. "So, are we going to run or not? We do have nationals to prepare for." The rest of the team looks at each other, unsure of what is going on, and whether or not they should go with what the Sprinter is saying.

"Heather, Michelle, and Nina, come over to the start line and we'll run it out to see who will represent our team for the hundred-yard dash." The three girls she mentioned step forward. I smile when I realize why she has chosen them. They are the ones who have been harassing and picking on her the most. The Sprinter is doing better than Tigerclaw already. The three girls take their place at the start line on the track field, looking over at each other and the Sprinter, confused and concerned. They're probably thinking that this has to be some kind of weird joke or a dream. I laugh as I think to myself, you're going to wish that this was just a dream.

The Sprinter takes her time making it to the starting line, giving herself the pleasure of making her cruel teammates wait. Once she does get there, only a second passes before one of the other team members yells out for them to start and the Sprinter is off like a bullet. As she passes the other racers, she pushes them down roughly, laughing as they fall and cry out before she makes it around the track in a few seconds and passes over the finish line with a smile on her face and a saunter in her step.

"Anybody else want to take me on?" The other team members look at her with horror at what has just happened. I think it is now obvious to all of them what has happened. They have realized that their old teammate is now under my control. None of them step forward to her challenge, in fact, some of them are beginning to back away. The Sprinter sees this, but she is not happy about it. "Come on!

Don't tell me that all of you are scared!" The Sprinter laughs in all of their faces. "I should have guessed that you all were weak. I was always the one who carried the team, you guys always just lagged behind me!" One of the other girls finally steps forward, her fear being outmatched by her anger at the Sprinter's words.

"We are just as valuable to this team as you are Cheyanne! Don't act like we aren't!" I can feel the Sprinter's hands clenching into fists at her side.

"My name is the Sprinter now! Don't you *ever* forget it!" A few of the team members back a few steps away at her scream. The Sprinter calms herself down before she speaks again. "If you think you're so valuable to the team, why don't you prove it." The girl who spoke up walks over to the starting line beside the Sprinter as the Sprinter smiles at her, knowing that she will beat her, knowing that nobody will ever be able to run faster than her or look down on her again.

When another member of the team tells them to go the Sprinter runs down the track course faster than any other living being ever could. I watch the world pass by through her eyes, loving the view of everything zipping by her. As she makes it over the finish line she tries to slow down her pace, but she was running too fast to slow down quickly. One of the first rules of running, you can't stop immediately, you have to slow down first. Her quick moving feet try to catch on the ground, but she is still moving forward. The Sprinter looks up, realizing what is happening. She isn't going to stop before she hits something. We both see what she's about to hit, a wall of the school. The two of us close our eyes getting ready for impact. Even though I won't feel anything since I am just viewing this from her head, I still close my eyes, knowing that what will happen won't be pleasant. My entire body tenses as I wait for the crash that I know will come.

Chapter Fifteen

Colomba-
The Sprinter

Finishing up a test, I stand up to place it on the teacher's desk before returning to my seat and sitting down to try and get a few minutes of rest before the class is over. I have been having to do this for a while now since I barely get any sleep anymore because of my nightmares with the Crow. As soon as my eyes have closed, they snap open again. I am having that feeling again, the feeling that something bad is about to happen. All thought of my exhaustion leaves me as I look around to try and figure out where the danger is coming from. Nothing looks unusual though. Everyone is just working on their tests silently, trying to figure out the answers. The door to the classroom is closed, and it doesn't feel as if the danger will be coming from there. My body freezes in terror and my eyes grow wide as I suddenly realize something. The danger is coming from behind me.

I pull a student sitting beside me to the ground just in time as something crashes through the wall behind us. Looking up, I see a girl dressed in a form- fitting outfit of red and black with dark shades covering their eyes. Their outfit almost looks like something you would see in an alien movie. It is so bizarre looking that I am almost tempted to laugh. Every inch of them is covered by their costume, only their mouth can be seen. This strange person moves their head from side to side, examining the room with eyes hidden behind the shades, but this only makes their gaze more frightening.

This person brushes the rubble from their costume as the other students run away in terror. It is obvious what has happened, the Crow has created another monster and they don't want to be around to see what this person will do. I stay behind, too curious to make myself move. The girl looks at me, wondering why I didn't run away like everyone else.

"Who are you?" I ask them softly, almost in a whisper. The strange girl gives me a sly smile.

"I am the Sprinter." I gasp in shock when my mind suddenly remembers that nickname. That nickname was given to someone because of their amazing ability to run faster than anybody else in this school. Someone who everybody respected because of this talent, Cheyanne. When I look up at her now, I don't see that same person that I had admired before. In front of me stands someone who is consumed by their misery, someone who has been influenced by the Crow. He must have seen how she was being picked on since she wouldn't have been able to run in nationals because of her broken leg. He must have heard all the insulting words people have said to her and decided to make her his next victim. Looking down at her newly healed leg I can easily guess what the Crow has promised her so that she will do whatever he says. He gave her back her leg, as well as super speed, so that she can be the best on the team again. When I look at her, I can only hope that I can figure out a way to convince her to give up these powers when it is something that I know she truly wants.

Without another word, the Sprinter runs straight through the wall again, creating another massive hole. This makes a problem though, a few pieces of rubble fall, and I know what is about to happen. I let out a horrified scream and try to leap out of the way just as the rest of the wall and part of the ceiling crumbles around me. Its tumbles down in an earsplitting roar and then all is silent.

Coughing from the dust in the air, I open my eyes to see that I had missed getting hit by practically everything that had fallen, but my foot is now pinned by chunks of rock from the wall. Somehow, I don't feel any pain in my foot. Because of this I don't think I am hurt badly, but when I try to pull it out, I can't do it. I am trapped.

I try to lift the rocks that are pinning my foot, but I can't even budge them, they are way too heavy. I breathe a sigh of relief. No problem, I'll just transform into Silver Dove and I can lift it easy peasy. I am about to place my hand over my pin when I hear several people coming into the room. Turning around, I see three students running in, terrified looks on their faces as they stare at my leg.

"Are you hurt?!" They all ask me, and I keep repeating to them that I am fine, but they keep asking me. They all look too frightened to be paying attention to what I'm saying. All three of them try to lift the rocks that are pinning me, but nothing seems to work. I try to beg them to go find help, but none of them listen. They are too busy trying to lift that rock. I have to force back so much anger so that I won't scream at them. I know that they are just scared right now, that's why they're not listening to me. I just need to help them calm down, then they will do what I say and go get help. If they would just go away I could get myself free as Silver Dove.

A minute of this craziness passes by until a shriek makes them all stop. One of the girls who had been trying to lift the rock had been the one to scream. She is staring at the doorway to the classroom. We all look at the doorway to see something that makes my heart stop in terror, the Crow.

Everyone in the room freezes as we stare at the Crow who watches us from the doorway. We all stay in that position in silence until he says one simple word, "Leave."

The other students practically leap to their feet as they rush to the door.

"Wait! Please don't leave me behind!" I shout out to the retreating students, but they don't listen to my begging. The three students run away from me and out the door, leaving me behind with a monster. I feel my eyes growing wide in my fear as I try to pull my leg out, but I still can't move it. The Crow moves closer and closer to me. He is moving slowly toward me, as if he is trying to frighten me, which he is succeeding at. I try harder and harder to get my leg free, but nothing works. In fact, it seems to make it worse. The more I move my leg, the more the rubble on top shifts and covers more of my leg. My breathing is hard and heavy in my fear. In my head I keep repeating the same things. I need to get away from him. I can't let him near me. Does he know that I am Silver Dove? Is that why he has come to me now while I am weak? Should I just transform now to defend myself even though he would easily figure out my secret identity? If I did transform now, could I win?

When he is only a few feet away from me I stop trying to pull at my leg, knowing that it is useless. Instead, I just look up at him. Looking into the face of my fate. In an instant, he creates two of his shadow dogs and I let out a gasp of fear. The two dogs tower over me, growling furiously. I breathe in strained gasps, knowing that I am about to be ripped to shreds by a maniac's demonic dogs. I know that I could transform into Silver Dove right now, but I have the feeling that he would still take me down before I am able to try and defend myself. After he would be done killing me, he would then know who I really am and then take out my family and friends as revenge. I can't let that happen no matter how scared I am right now. Closing my eyes, I accept my fate. The dogs let out a bark and I can almost sense them lunging at me. My muscles stiffen as I get ready for my death, but it doesn't come.

Opening my eyes, I see that the dogs have dug their teeth into the rocks and are ripping them apart as easily as if they were pieces of paper. The dogs spit rocks from their mouths, and before I know it the massive rock has disappeared above my foot. Cautiously I bring it closer to me, not wanting my foot anywhere near the ferocious dogs who are strong enough to break apart rocks. The Crow could easily see my discomfort with the dogs since he gives a simple wave of his hand and they disappear since they are no longer needed. With them gone I am now left alone again with the Crow.

The two of us stare at each other for a moment. He is looking into my eyes while I am looking into his mask in confusion and fear. I can barely make out his eyes beneath the mask. His face is turned a weird way so that I can't see them clearly. It's almost as if he is trying to hide them from me. From what I can see, they are dark eyes. Eyes full of misery. It feels as if an eternity passes before he finally breaks the silence between the two of us.

"Can you walk?" His deep voice sends a shiver down my spine. The Crow's voice is frightening, almost like what you would expect to hear in a nightmare. When I had met him last, when he first showed up at my school, he had spoken to me then, but this seems different. Back then he was yelling at me and he was full of anger. Somehow this calmer voice he is using is scarier. Maybe it's because he is so close to me that it seems more frightening. I don't understand why this feels so much more terrifying. It takes all of my courage to respond to him.

"I don't know." I respond, barely above a whisper. He kneels down in front of me and extends his hand to try and examine my foot, but I pull it away from him, afraid of what he might do. The Crow looks up at me calmly. Now that he is kneeling down, his mask is now only around a foot away from my face.

"Don't be afraid, I've taken some classes on basic first aid. I just want to check and see if you are hurt." Without letting my eyes leave him, I extend my leg out so that he can hold it in his hand. The Crow has very large hands, my foot looks so tiny in comparison. If I wasn't so scared, I would laugh about it. His long fingers carefully examine my foot and ankle before he speaks again. "I don't think that it's broken or sprained, it may just hurt for a little while. You'll be fine." He almost sounds relieved when he says this, as if he was worried about me.

He stares at me for a moment, and I feel really uncomfortable by it. I actually have to look away from his gaze. It felt as if I was being examined and I don't like it. Without giving me any kind of explanation, like a gentleman would do, he simply lifts me into his arms and starts carrying me out of the room. I am very tempted to punch him in the face, but I know that probably wouldn't end well.

"What on earth are you doing?" I ask him this even though I'm a bit afraid to know the answer. He doesn't even look at me as he responds.

"I'm taking you to a place where you will be safe until this is all over." The Crow keeps walking down the hallway while people run at the sight of him. None of them bothering to try and save me from his clutches. I look at the Crow, but I am still confused.

"Why are you helping me?" He stops walking for a moment, as if he is suddenly realizing what he is doing and is confused by it too.

"I'm here to punish the people who deserve it, you don't. You're one of the few good people I have seen in this school. I wouldn't want you to get hurt when you are not the one who needs to be punished." He says this as if it is supposed to make sense.

"We must go to different schools since I know of a lot of good people here." He chuckles softly at my words.

"We *must* go to different schools since I can only think of a few good people that go here." What does this guy live through every day that makes him see the world as such a terrible place? When I think of my life, I am surrounded by good people and happy moments. Does the Crow have any good people in his life? Does he have any happy moments? Is this why he is acting like this with his new powers?

I want to ask him these questions, but I am too afraid. I am in the arms of my enemy; how else should I feel? Since this is the closest I've ever been to him, I am almost tempted to rip his mask off so I can finally see who he is. To see who has been haunting my nightmares for so long. I want to do this, but that would be a terrible idea. He is being kind to me right now. If I took off his mask, he might not be so nice anymore. Maybe if I knew who he really is then I could help him so that he won't feel as if he has to give people superpowers so that they can get revenge and everything. I could help him see that life can be better, you just need some help. I could do that, I could help him, but I know that he wouldn't listen. He doesn't want to listen.

A terrible thought flashes through my mind. Do I even want to know who he really is? He said that he knows that I am a good person. Does that mean that I know him? Or has he just seen me in the hallways or something? I'm not sure, but if I did know who is behind that mask, would I be happy to know who it is? Could he be a friend of mine from class? Would I be disappointed with the person behind the mask? Or could I find a way to forgive him if I could see who he is? When I look up at that mask, I can't find the answer to any of those questions.

The Crow walks on in silence until he reaches the teacher's lounge. He opens the door to find one of the teachers curled up in a corner crying, probably terrified by what is going on the with Sprinter. She looks up with red eyes from her tears to gasp in horror. The two of them stare at each other for a moment before he gives her an order.

"Get out." She follows his order without question. Running out the door while he walks to the other side of the room where a couch is sitting against the wall. Gently, he sets me down on the couch. "Stay here until this is all over. You will be safe, I promise." He starts walking away.

"Wait, stop!" I try to stand up, but I let out a cry because of the pain in my foot which makes me sit back down. He turns back to look at me, and I have the sudden feeling that he wants to come back and comfort me in my pain.

"I know you want to stop me, but it won't work. I need to do this." He practically marches out of the room and closes the door behind him. As soon as the door has closed, a shadow dog appears in the room. My body stiffens in terror, afraid that if I move it might notice me. The dog doesn't really seem to care about me though, it just uses its massive shoulder to push several filing cabinets against the door, blocking me in, before it disappears like the shadow it is.

Forgetting the pain in my foot, in my fear I limp to the blocked door and bang my fists against the filing cabinets.

"*Let me out! You can't keep me in here like this! Please let me out!*" Even though I beg him to let me out, I only hear silence on the other side of the door. What just happened? The Crow protected me? What does this mean? Wait, I don't have time to think about this, I need to step into action.

Placing my hand over my pin, I say the magic

words, "Peaceful warrior." I close my eyes, and in an instant, I have transformed into Silver Dove. Opening my wings out wide, I smile to myself, it's time to get some work done. I wait a few minutes before I use my super strength to push the filing cabinets away and rush out the door. I had to wait to make sure that the Crow had left before leaving that room or else he would easily figure out that I am really Silver Dove. He would have to be really dumb to not be able to figure that out after I walk out of the same blocked room that Silver Dove hadn't been in before.

I open up my wings and take off down the hallway. I don't search for the Crow. I know that he must have gone back into hiding and it would only waste my time to try and search him. Instead I look for the Sprinter. I know that she won't be hiding from me. She is the one I need to fight. If I want things to return to normal I need to defeat her, and I need to do it fast. In my exhausted state, I don't know how long I can last in a fight before my powers fade away.

Chapter Sixteen

Luis-
Saving Colomba

I hear her banging on the other side of the door, begging me to let her out. More than anything, I want to let her out and tell her that everything will be alright, but I know I can't. To protect her I need to keep her out of harm's way. I would never forgive myself if she got hurt because of one of the people I have given superpowers accidently did something to her. I would give up on all my plans if something like that were to happen. I would give it up and use my powers to make sure that everyone is safe, especially Colomba. I wouldn't even bother with the bullies anymore. I would just make sure that nobody is getting physically hurt.

Earlier, when I was watching what was happening through the Sprinter's eyes, I watched as the Sprinter crashed through the wall and then ran back out to return to the track court. Behind her, she could hear Colomba scream in terror as the wall collapsed. The Sprinter wanted to go back to try and help, but I told her that I would take care of it. I know that the Sprinter was probably confused as to why I was so concerned with a random person in our school while we were trying to complete our mission, but I didn't provide any kind of explanation. I had to leave the Sprinter's point of view so that I could see out of my own eyes. I ran out of the bathroom I had locked myself in without any thought of what might happen to me. With my powers I'm not invincible. Silver Dove was the one lucky enough to get that power, so anybody could have come up behind me and attack and I wouldn't have been able to really do anything to defend myself since I don't have super strength either. Why did Silver Dove get all the useful powers? I could make shadow dogs to defend myself, but it takes a lot of concentration to make those things and it's hard to think when you are getting attacked. I learned that a long time ago when Alex first started beating me up after school when we were still little kids.

I probably should have made some shadow dogs to protect me as I was running to the classroom that Colomba was in, but I was too terrified that she might have been hurt to even think about doing that. It's hard to think when you are afraid that someone you care about might be in danger or in pain. As I ran into the room, I saw that she was surrounded by three other students, all of them trying to lift a few huge rocks that were pinning her foot down. She didn't seem to be in pain though despite all of the rocks, I breathed a sigh of relief when I saw that. One of the students must have heard my sigh since they looked up and let out a scream of horror when they saw me. They all stared at me like deer in the headlights, even Colomba. It hurt to see how scared she was of me, but I tried to not let that show. I told them to leave, and they all ran off like frightened children. They left Colomba alone with me, which she did not seem happy about.

After I had examined her leg and saw that she wasn't hurt, I knew I had to get her out of there fast. She was almost killed by those falling rocks, I couldn't let something like that happen again. Picking her up, I started carrying her out of the classroom. Something else she wasn't happy about. She looked like she wanted to punch me in the face when I did that. Knowing she does martial arts; I was a bit scared that she would. Thankfully she showed me mercy and let me carry her. I could feel her entire body trembling in fear as I held her. I tried not to look at her since I didn't want her to recognize my eyes.

As I set her down on the couch in the

teacher's lounge and started walking away, she tried to get up and follow me, but she let out a small cry of pain when she tried to stand on her hurt foot. I wanted to go back to her and comfort her, but I knew that if I did then I would want to stay with her until this is all over and I need to watch over the Sprinter to make sure that she is doing her job right. Instead of going to her like I really wanted, I left the room and got one of my shadow dogs to block the door with some filing cabinets so that nobody could get in or out without my help. I plan on returning to get those cabinets out of the way as soon as this is all over, as soon as I have won. That way I can make sure that Colomba doesn't get involved or hurt.

I walk away from the door now, her begging starting to fade as I get farther and farther from the door. Walking into an empty classroom, I lock the door and close my eyes so that I can see through the Sprinter's eyes again. She is running around the track field now, knocking down several of her teammates as she passes them.

Even though things are going well for her, just as I had planned, I still don't feel happy about it right now. I had felt Colomba practically shivering with terror as I had carried her. I have never seen anybody so afraid before. More than anything, I want her opinion of me to change. Now that I have helped her though, and kept her out of danger, maybe now she will realize that I'm not such a bad guy. I am capable of being good too despite the way she has been saying bad things about me before. My new soldier isn't even acting scary like my last one, Tigerclaw, had done. The Sprinter is just showing off her new speed to the rest of the track team, easily convincing them to let her rejoin the team. Sure, she is pushing them down as she runs past them and I will let her get some revenge on some of the other people who were so mean to her after she hurt her leg, but it won't be as bad as before. I will make sure of that. I can't just create these superpowered people just to scare people, I need them to teach everyone a lesson. I don't want to be seen as the bad guy.

The Sprinter is running with the rest of the team now, leaving them in the dust. I let my words go through her mind.

Sprinter, I am going to tell you something important, so I need you to listen very carefully.

Of course. Whatever you want I will do it. She sounds eager to do anything I tell her. Good, that's what I want in my soldiers, obedience.

I don't want you to go anywhere near the teacher's lounge. I have placed something important there and I don't want it to be disturbed. If anything should happen to it, I will take away your powers and I won't give them back, do you understand? There is no hesitation before she responds to me.

Yes Crow, I understand. I will do whatever you say. Nobody will go into that room without regretting it. I feel my lips pulling up into a smile behind my mask, I should have chosen this girl as my soldier ages ago.

Good, remember that Sprinter. If you do what I say then you will get everything you desire, go against me and you will lose everything. That is a promise, and I always keep my promises.

I think that I have finally found my perfect soldier. First off, she is loyal. She said that she wouldn't go into that room without any questions as to why I asked her that or what is in the room. That's probably the most important thing I should look for in my soldiers, I need to remember that for the next soldier I will create. Second, she is determined to do what needs to be done. I think she would do anything to accomplish what she wants in life. And third, she is getting these things done. She is getting her revenge on the people who had turned on her in her hour of need. She is making everyone fear her. That's what I need to make everyone stop picking on each other. Make them afraid of bullying other people and bullying stops, simple as that. Sad that Silver Dove doesn't realize the genius of my plan.

I watch with a smile on my face as the Sprinter runs across the field, knocking people to the ground easily. Everything is going perfectly. Soon this will all be over, and I will finally come out the winner.

Chapter Seventeen

Colomba-
Fighting the
Sprinter

Flying out the back door of the school, I head straight to the track field where I can see the Sprinter running with the track team. They are all trying to race her, but they can't even get close to her since she is moving so fast. She looks like she's barely even trying to beat them while the team is gasping for breath in their exhaustion. I also see her knock them down as she passes them, I can even hear her laughing as she does this. What has happened to Cheyanne to make her so cold? Before all of this happened, before she broke her leg, she was nice to everyone. I never heard her say a mean word to anyone and now she's pushing people down and letting the Crow influence her. It fills my heart with pain to know that someone so kind has been influenced and changed into something else.

"Come on you guys, are you tired already? I thought you said that you were good runners." One of the team members glares at her and manages to say some angry words in between her gasps for air.

"Of course we're tired! We've been running nonstop for almost an hour and you keep challenging us to race you!" The Sprinter shakes her head, smiling at them.

"I didn't think you guys would be this weak. I should have expected it though since you guys have always depended on me to win every race." The entire team glares at her, but none of them say a thing. I think that deep down they all know that what she's saying is true. Cheyanne was always the star of the team, the one who always lead them to victory. The rest of the team just stuck with her so that they could share in the glory of being on such a good team. Without Cheyanne, they would have been nothing. "Well, if you guys aren't going to give me a challenge then I'll just run by myself." She runs away from them, faster than any human could run, leaving the team far behind.

Forcing my wings to fly faster, I manage to catch up to her and fly next to her. The Sprinter looks over to her side and notices me flying beside her.

"*What are you doing here?!*" She yells out in anger. I point to myself sarcastically.

"Oh me? Well I'm just here to warn you about that tree." She narrows her eyes at me in confusion.

"What tree?" She looks in front of herself to quickly realize which tree I was talking about. The Sprinter doesn't even have a chance to stop before she runs straight into the tree. With her speed and force, she crashes straight through the tree with an ear-splitting boom. Splinters and bits of wood fly all over the place as she tumbles to the ground, rolling over the demolished pieces of timber. I hear her moaning as I land only a few feet away from her. As she picks herself back up from the pile of wood chips, her entire body is stiff in her anger, her hands clench into fists at her side.

"Why are you here? I'm not doing anything bad like what Tigerclaw did. You don't have the right to mess with me when all I'm doing is running!"

"You're not doing anything bad? Really? Scaring people and demolishing part of the school isn't anything bad? I think I know a few people who would disagree with you." The Sprinter scowls at me while she brushes off the dust and splinters from the demolished tree on her costume using quick motions with her hands.

"*Don't try telling me what to do!*" The Sprinter yells at me, obviously trying to avoid the question I just asked her. "You said that you are here to help everyone in this school, well I'm not one of those people that needs your help. I can take care of myself." I can't help but chuckle at her words.

"And when you say that you can take care of yourself that means that you need the Crow to give you powers and fix your leg so that you can do all this damage and scare a bunch of people." Her hands clench into fists at her side again and I can bet that she is glaring at me from behind those shades.

"Just shut up, I don't want to talk to you anymore!" Without another word, she races off toward the school, leaving me in her dust. I sigh to myself as I try to forget how tired I am already before I open up my wings to chase after her.

Flying as fast as I can, I rush toward her, slowly gaining on her. She doesn't even look back as she runs. She doesn't think that I will follow her, or she doesn't think I can catch up. Either way, she is in for a big surprise. As soon as I am right behind her, I grab her by the back of her costume and immediately stop. Her legs fly out from under her as she falls onto her back completely stunned. She moans softly in pain as she tries to pick herself up in her stunned state. She looks up at me with a surprised expression as she sees me standing over her.

The Sprinter practically leaps to her feet as she takes off again. Before I can even open my wings to chase her again I feel something rush toward me and then I am thrown backward, landing hard on my back. I let out a moan as I realize what just happened. The Sprinter had run past me and punched me in the face while running at super speed. Wow that was not fun! That was not fun at all.

As I lay on the ground, I am fighting the urge to just stay there and close my eyes. My body feels as if it is made of lead. I can barely move a muscle. I want to sleep so badly. My grandma has warned me that if I get too tired as Silver Dove then I transform back into my usual self. I need to end this fight and I need to end it now before I am exposed.

Picking myself back up, I am thrown back down again by another punch to the face. I feel my fists tighten in frustration as I try to pick myself up for the third time. This time though, I have a plan. When I am up on my knees, as soon as I feel the gust of wind on my face that tells me that she is coming at me, I open my wings suddenly and feel someone trip over them. Looking behind me, I can see the Sprinter tumbling across the ground before landing in the pile of wood bits from the tree that she exploded earlier when she ran into it.

I start marching toward her as she picks herself up, brushing the bits of wood off of her costume. When she sees me coming, she runs off again in the blink of an eye. I groan to myself, "Oh *come on!*"

Flying after her, I feel my muscles starting to

weaken. I am getting more tired than I have ever been in my entire life. I shake my head, trying to get rid of the sleepiness. I can't let myself get tired. I can't let them win. I force myself to fly faster, wanting to get to her quicker so I can end this sooner. In my condition I can't do this all day. From what I can feel, I can only last another couple of minutes before I pass out.

As I chase her around the track field of the school, I start creeping closer and closer to her. Reaching out my hand, I latch myself onto her and wrap my wings around her. The two of us fall to the ground together, both of us kicking and punching each other as we do. When we both stop rolling from the fall I make sure that I am on top of her, sending out as many punches as I can while she sends out punches so fast that I can't even see them. The Sprinter sends out one wicked punch that sends me flying back and she leaps back to her feet, immediately rushing toward me to hit me again. Blocking her strike, I swing one of my wings forward, knocking her off her feet again. As I walk over to her she doesn't pick herself back up again, she stays on the ground. When I am standing above her, I can see that her body is shaking, almost as if she is crying.

"All I wanted to do was run." The Sprinter whimpers as she looks up at me. She lifts up her shades so that I can see tears forming in her eyes.

"That is what has always made me happy. I loved being a part of the track team. It was the best thing to ever happen to me. I never felt more free than when I was running with the team and winning matches. When they said we got into nationals, it was a dream come true." The tears are now falling down her face. "I didn't want to get hurt, couldn't they see that?! I wanted to run, that's what I've always wanted!" She covers her face with her hands for a moment before she looks back up at me, wiping the tears away from her face.

"Once I got hurt though, nobody cared about me. They all hated me as if I had done something wrong. All of my friends left me as if I was nothing to them. I just wanted to get them back by showing them that I am faster than ever, and I can still beat them. That's what they always wanted from me, to help them win. If I could just help them win one more time at nationals then I would never have to be afraid of losing them again." As fresh tears start falling down her face, I kneel down beside her, my arm wrapping around her shoulder.

"If they left you when you needed them the most, then why are you trying to get them back? It doesn't seem like they were your true friends." She looks up at me with hopeless eyes.

"Because they're the only friends I have." I am almost stunned by her words, unable to believe that she could be so blind. What goes on in this girl's head to make her think that those girls on the track team are the only friends she has in the world?

"Your only friends? Do you honestly not see how many people care about you in this school?" She stares at me as if she is unsure if I am telling her the truth. "You are kind to everyone at this school, and so many people admire you. You are not as alone as you think." She quickly turns her face away from me.

"But, when I got hurt, everyone turned against me. Nobody helped me."

"Think back, was it really everyone who did this or was it only a few who hurt you by saying all of those things?" She looks off into the distance as she thinks.

"I guess it was only a few people who did that, but only one person was nice to me. Everyone else avoided me like I was a slimy frog or something equally gross."

"Maybe they were just afraid to be kind to you. It's hard to stand next to the person that is getting picked on. Maybe you can be an example to them and stand beside others who are getting hurt. You have always been someone people look up to in this school, maybe you can make a difference that way. Maybe you can be the change that this school needs" She finally looks up at me, a smile coming through as the tears start to fade.

"Do you really think that everything will be

alright for me, even without my friends on the team?" I nod at her, smiling in my honesty.

"Of course, it may not be easy, but nothing worth a lot in life is ever easy." I hug her gently. "Are you ready to let go of this power that the Crow has given you? Are you ready to get rid of all your pain?" I can feel her take a deep, shaking breath in my arms.

"Yes, yes I'm ready." I let go of her so that I can look her in the eyes.

"Before you do, there is something I want to ask you." Her eyes narrow in confusion.

"What is it?"

"Can the Crow hear us right now?" She stops for a moment to think before she nods, still confused.

"Yes, the Crow sees everything through my eyes and hears everything I can hear." My smile goes wider.

"Good because I need to speak to him." I look her right in the eyes, knowing that I am also looking into the eyes of the Crow, wherever he is hiding.

"Crow, I know you are watching us somehow, so I will tell you this, you don't frighten me anymore." I think back to only an hour or so ago when he saved me from being pinned by those rocks. "I have seen who you truly are. You are not the monster you are pretending to be. You are better than that!" I take a deep breath to help me find the courage to say what I know needs to be said. "I do not fear you. I pity you." I tighten my fists at my side to try and prevent my hands from shaking. I may not feel afraid of him, but I am afraid that he might do something bad in reaction to what I'm saying. "You are lost, and you feel as if nobody can help you. When you are ready to accept the fact that I am here to help you, then we can talk. We can work this out. There is no more need for violence." I let my voice fade away with the wind, hoping that the Crow really is watching, hoping that he heard me.

I don't know how many times I will have to say it, but I really do want this to end peacefully. I want to help him so that he can be happy too. I know that he is probably miserable the way he is now. That's how it sounded when I first met him about four months ago, and that's how he sounded only a little while ago when he was talking to me as Colomba. I don't want him to feel that way anymore. I may have to tell him this a million times before he believes me, but one day I will make him believe me. I will make him believe the truth.

Bringing my hand over the dove emblem on my armor, I say the magic words, "Bring peace little dove." The dove flies off my armor and flies higher into the air until it is just a shining star in the bright sky. I close my eyes, and when I open them again, all of the damage that the Sprinter had caused is now gone.

I glance down at the Sprinter, who is staring up at me in awe. She is amazed that I was able to show courage by saying that about the Crow when he could attack from anywhere. She closes her eyes and in the blink of an eye she is back to her usual self, she is Cheyanne again. Something catches her attention though, she looks away from me, her eyes narrowing in confusion. Cheyanne stares down at her leg in complete shock, as if he can't believe what she's seeing. There is no longer a huge pink cast on her leg. Slowly, she bends her leg and starts moving it around, probably testing to see if she feels any pain or not.

"My leg... it's healed?" I smile down at her, trying to figure out a way to explain this to her without sounding confusing.

"I have a great deal of magic within me. I'm sure that you know that one of my powers is to fix whatever was broken in my battles with the Crow and those he controls. In this instance, I just let my magic fix one other thing as well." She stares up at me completely confused, well apparently my explanation failed.

"Why would you do that for me after all of the stuff I just did? I don't deserve it. I don't deserve anything from you." I sigh as I kneel down beside her.

"It's not about whether or not you deserve it

because of what you did as the Sprinter. You just fell for the Crow's trick, that's all. Someone has done that already before you and I am sure that there will be many other people who will fall for the same trick. You are a good person, I know that. I have seen your kindness many times when you are at school. You help others and you never look down on anyone despite the fact that everyone looks up to you. That is who you really are, that is the person who deserves to be given a second chance and have their leg fixed." A tear falls down her face as she smiles at me with pure gratitude.

"Thank you, thank you so much Silver Dove. I can never tell you how much this means to me." I place my hand on her shoulder as I smile back at her.

"There is no need to thank me. I am just doing what's right." Standing up, I start walking away from her. When I am a few feet away, I turn back. "Just promise me something though, before I go."

"What is it?" Her eyes are eager, ready to do whatever I ask of her in her gratitude.

"Now that you are healed, the people who hurt you may try to be your friends again. I just want to ask you to be wise. It's best not to be friends with people would turn on you so quickly." I smile a little sadly at her, knowing that what I'm asking will be difficult. The people who turned on her were the ones she considered her best friends. I am asking her, no *begging* her, to be smart and not be friends with them anymore since they weren't true friends to her.

Cheyanne looks away from me and I know that she is thinking about what I just said. I can only hope that she pays attention to my words and takes my advice to heart. I would hate to come back to school and see her with those same people who would hurt her again if she got injured or anything bad happened to her. She is a kind girl who deserves better friends than them. I want her to have real friends, friends who will stay by her side when she needs them the most, people who care about her like true friends do.

I am about to leave her when she stops me.

"Silver Dove?" I smile down at her.

"Yes?"

"Before, when I still had those powers, the Crow told me something weird that might be important."

"What is it?"

"He told me not to go into the teacher's lounge. He said that something very important was in there and I shouldn't mess with it if I wanted to keep my powers." I feel my eyes growing wide behind my mask. What did he mean by that? I was in that room before I transformed into Silver Dove. There wasn't anything really important in there. I doubt he had put anything there before he dropped me off there since that teacher was in the room when we got there, and I doubt she would stay in the room if she saw the Crow putting something in there. Was that "something" he wanted protected me? Am I what he considered to be so important? I don't understand, what is going on?

Cheyanne is staring at my confused expression with curiosity, I try to make her feel better with a simple lie.

"Thank you very much Cheyanne, I will look into that to make sure that everything is alright."

I turn away again, I open my wings and take flight. I search through the hallways for an empty room so that I can transform back into my normal self. As I search, I feel my heart breaking for Cheyanne, knowing the choice she has to make. I hold back my emotions as I enter the empty classroom that I had left my backpack in and transform back into my normal self. Taking a deep breath to hold back my pity and pain for Cheyanne, I grab my bag and head back into the hallway so that I can head for the bus since school ended about ten minutes ago. As I go, I try and figure out what on earth the Crow could have meant by saying that there was something important hidden in the teacher's lounge. Even though I try to think of something, I am still left clueless. Nothing comes into my mind about what that special thing could be, nothing except me.

Chapter Eighteen

Luis-
A New
Agreement

No, *no, NO!!!!* Why did this happen?! Why did it have to end like this?! Everything was going so well, why did the Sprinter back down? She was impressing her teammates and making them look pathetic compared to her. She even got her revenge, shoving down and scaring all the other team members who abandoned her when she got hurt, making them feel as defeated as she did when they left her alone after being injured. The Sprinter gave them everything they deserved, but then Silver Dove had to show up and ruin everything!

I almost feel like crying right now. I feel so pathetic. I am more powerful than Silver Dove, Shadow told me that, so why am I getting beaten by her all the time? How can I be defeated by someone weaker than me who usually just talks my soldiers into quitting instead of forcing them to? As I transform into my normal self, I place my hand over my Crow Medal and Shadow appears on the counter in front of me. She doesn't say anything. She only looks at me as if she is waiting for something. I glare down at her.

"I don't want to hear it right now Shadow." She doesn't seem surprised by my words. In fact, she is perfectly calm.

"What don't you want to hear Master?" She sounds as if she already knows the answer, but she is just asking this question so that I can say what needs to be said.

"I don't want to hear you say that I shouldn't have done this, that Silver Dove was right, and that I should just give up on all of this and join her side. You've said all of that to me a million times before, I don't need to hear it again." For a minute, Shadow doesn't say anything to me, she is calmly evaluating the situation.

"Strange that you have all of this memorized, yet you still don't listen to what I have to say." I feel my hands clench into fists at my side. "If you didn't want to hear what I have to say, then why did you summon me here?" I look away from her, suddenly feeling embarrassed.

"I just wanted someone to talk to. I was just

defeated by my enemy, again, so I just want to say something to someone and you're the only one I can talk to about all of this."

"You want to talk to me because you think that I can understand?" I laugh coldly.

"You could never understand. You don't know what it's like to be afraid all the time. To wish that you were somewhere else, *anywhere* else except here! I'm tired of feeling this way and I don't want anyone else to feel like this! I will end this no matter what I have to do! I will do anything to make sure that nobody gets hurt again!" Shadow stares at me with both pride and pity.

"You can't promise that to anyone Master. You can't promise that nobody will ever be hurt again because that is a part of life. Everyone gets hurt no matter how prepared or safe you try to make yourself. Nobody can live a life without at least a little pain." I look away from her, not wanting to see the pity in her eyes.

"I know, but that doesn't mean I can't try to make things better for the other kids like me." I hear a flutter of wings and Shadow perches on my shoulder. I look back up at her and for a moment the two of us look into each others' eyes. In her gaze I see her motherly love toward me.

"It would be impossible for me to say that I don't respect what you want to do, even though I may be against how you are doing it. I want to ask you to make an agreement with me." I feel my eyes narrow, suddenly confused.

"What kind of agreement do you have in mind?"

"I believe that we should make the agreement that we will never disagree about this again. I know that your heart is in the right place, so if you believe that this is the way to reach your goal then I will follow you with all my heart despite what I believe. You are my master, the one who holds my medal, and I know that I chose you well when your uncle gave the medal to you. I know that you will make the world a better place." I smile at her, feeling as if she really does understand me.

"I think I can agree to that." She nods her head at me, and I have the feeling that, if she was human, she would be smiling at me.

"Good, then I will follow you until the ends of the earth. I will help you in any way I can." I gently stroke the feathers on her wings while she rubs her face against mine. Without saying anything, we understand each other. We are no longer just two beings stuck with each other, we are truly friends. She is a friend who will help me finally bring my ideas to life. Every other friend that I have ever had (besides Colomba and Nat) have abandoned me when they figured out how much I get picked on. I know now that Shadow will never abandon me though. I have finally found a true friend.

Chapter Nineteen

Colomba-
New Questions

As I head down the hallway to head to my bus, everyone swarms out of the classrooms, talking excitedly about what just happened between me and the Sprinter. While everyone else is laughing and hugging each other, happy that they survived another attack from the Crow, I remain silent, trying to figure out what Cheyanne had told me about the Crow wanting to protect something in the teacher's lounge.

He saved me from being trapped by those fallen rocks and then carried me to safety into that room. Am I the something special he wanted protected? Is that why he placed those filing cabinets in front of the door, so that nobody would come in and hurt me? I mean he did risk a lot to help me, am I special to him somehow? If I am, then why does he feel that way? I'm not one of his supporters, in fact I have never really said anything positive about him before, so why does he care? He told me when he was carrying me there that he thought of me as one of the few kind people in this school. Is that why he views me as something special, or is there something else? Does he really view kindness as something so rare that he has to protect one of the kind people he has met? How horribly does this guy view our school? It's kind of sad.

My thoughts are interrupted by a girl from my class, Megan, coming up behind me and placing her hand on my shoulder.

"Hey Colomba." I smile at her, trying to forget the nagging questions swirling around in my head.

"Hey Megan, what's up?" She comes up beside me and wraps arm around my shoulder, holding me close as if she is about to tell me an amazing secret. Megan leans in close to me and whispers in my ear.

"I heard about what happened between you and the Crow." I have to hold back a gasp of surprise. Does she know about me as Silver Dove?! Is that what she's talking about?!

"What are you talking about?" I ask in the calmest voice I can. Megan leans in closer, her lips almost touching my ear.

"I heard about how the Crow saved you from

having your leg being crushed under some rocks and then carrying you to safety. What happened there? Is there something going on between you and the Crow?" I feel both calmer, and also still afraid by what she has said. I need to stop being so paranoid about people figuring out I'm Silver Dove or else I'm going to have a heart attack one of these days. Those people who had tried to help get those rocks off me, and those other people who were in the hallway when he carried me, must have told everybody about what they saw. I feel my hands trembling at my side. What is everyone going to say about this? Are they going to hate me because the Crow helped me? I know that people are going to be at least curious and I'm going to be asked endless questions about what happened, but what if people see this as a sign that I am something to be afraid of, like the Crow?

"There's nothing going on, he just said that he didn't want to hurt an innocent person in his weird little crusade, so he decided to save me. That's all. Nothing else happened." Megan shakes her head at me, smiling as if she has caught me trying to pull a prank on her.

"C'mon Colomba, you know you can tell me, right? I won't tell anybody what you tell me. Your secret will stay safe with me." In the back of my mind, I have the feeling that what I say to her will be spread all through the school. My "secret" wouldn't be safe with her, especially if it was as interesting as she obviously hopes it will be. My heart is pounding in my chest now. She doesn't believe me. If someone I consider as a friend doesn't believe me then who else will?

"I swear nothing happened, he just saw that I was in trouble and he helped me. There is nothing more than that going on." Megan's smile grows bigger.

"Well I heard that you and the Crow are dating, that's why he saved you, or that you're working with him. Everybody has been saying that around the school. What do you think about that?" I move away from her, letting her arm that had been wrapped around my shoulders drop. I stare at her completely horrified. How could she think that I am dating the Crow? How could she think that I am helping him in any way? Why are people making up these lies?

"I think that's stupid!" My words come out meaner than I had planned, but I can't hide how much anger I have in me right now. "There is no way that I would help him hurt people like this. I would never help anyone like him. How could you even think that Megan?" She shrugs at me as if what she's saying isn't a big deal.

"Well that's just what everyone has been saying so I thought I would ask." My heart that had been pounding only seconds ago has now stopped.

Everyone thinks this? Everyone thinks that I am helping or dating the Crow? Is everyone nuts?! How could they think that?! I look at Megan, suddenly afraid.

"You can tell them that I would rather die than be with the Crow in any way." With that said, I walk away, heading straight for my bus. I can't listen to any more of that stupidity. What on earth was she thinking asking me that? I'm not crazy, why would I help the Crow? Everyone else must be crazy for thinking this.

I walk into the bus and sit down on a seat near the back. Leaning my head back, I close my eyes to try and relax after everything that has just happened, but I can't. My thoughts are swirling in my head faster than a whirlpool. I feel like I'm going to throw up. What am I going to do?

Trying to calm myself, I whisper in my mind that everybody will probably just forget about this in a few days or nobody will believe the rumors and it will all pass. Why would anybody believe anything so stupid anyway? I repeat this over and over again in my head, but the negative thoughts of those rumors spreading through the school just keep screaming at me.

It doesn't take long for one of my friends to show up. Luis sits down beside me, giving me a friendly greeting as he smiles down at me. Something about the way he is smiling makes me think that he is waiting for me to say something that would make him happy, but I keep my mouth shut. I do know something that would please him if he heard me say it, but I know that it would only cause more tension between the two of us.

I could tell him about how the Crow had saved me earlier when those rocks fell on me, but then he would try to convince me to join the Crow's side like he has been trying to do since the Crow first showed up. He wants that so badly, but I could never do that. I can't support him no matter what he does for me. Judging from how fast the rumor spread to Megan though I'm guessing that he will know about what happened between me and the Crow very soon. I can only hope that he won't bother me too much with it. Knowing Luis though, he would never let me hear the end of it until I tell him that I will support the Crow. I can only hope that the universe will be kind to me and these rumors won't last long, and Luis won't bug me too much about them.

Nat sits down on the seat in front of me and starts telling us all about a new movie that she wants to go see, and I am thankful for the distraction from what happened earlier. I lose myself in her story until the bus pulls up in front of my house. I don't want to leave my friends because I know that when I am alone in my house, I will start thinking all of those negative thoughts again and I won't be able to get my mind to shut up. I will make myself go nuts with thoughts of those rumors.

As I step off the bus and walk down my driveway to get to my house, I smile to myself. I'm thinking the only happy thought I've had in several hours. The Crow saved me when that rock was on top of my leg, he was actually worried enough about me to leave his hiding place to come and get me. Someone could have attacked him to stop the Sprinter from scaring everyone. Nobody was brave enough to do that, but he still risked it to help me.

The Crow isn't such a bad person, he actually cares about people and wants to help. He isn't a monster like I have been telling myself. I think about how I have seen him in my nightmares for the past four months. Always there to hurt me, to destroy me, but he protected me today. I have been thinking of him as something completely bad when he is really just like everyone else, full of both good and bad pieces. Nobody is ever just all good or all bad. I had forgotten that fact when I thought of the Crow. I thought of him more as a monster than a person. I almost feel a bit guilty to know that I thought of someone so terribly. Nobody deserves to be thought of the way I thought about the Crow. No one deserves to be thought of as a monster. Even though he has done some bad things before, he said that he thinks he is doing it for the right reasons.

I remember when I had asked my grandmother

why the pin would work for him when it only works for people with good hearts. She told me that sometimes good people do bad things because they think something good will happen because of it. That is what the Crow is doing. He is a good person trying to end the bullying at this school by forcing it to stop. He is not a monster, he is lost. Even though this is a sad thought, I still smile a bit because I know that when I lay my head down to sleep tonight I think that my dreams will be safe. I don't think that the Crow will be haunting my nightmares any time soon.

Chapter Twenty

Luis-
New Hope

When Colomba had come on the bus at the end of the day I had expected her to talk about how the Crow helped her when the Sprinter attacked the school. I wanted her to say that she had changed her mind about the Crow. That she doesn't see me as a monster anymore. She didn't even mention it! She acted as if it didn't happen. I won't let that disappoint me though. I know that I have planted some doubt in her head. She is now probably thinking that I might not be that bad. I might actually be the good guy here. I feel as if I could fly without my wings right now. I haven't felt this much hope in something for a long time.

Stepping into my bedroom, I close the door behind me. Placing my hand over my medal, Shadow appears on top of my windowsill.

"Hello Master. How are you? You seem very happy." She cocks her head to the side, confused by my happiness.

"And you happen to be right. I am pretty happy right now." Shadow flies off the windowsill to land on my shoulder.

"I am guessing that your happiness is related to the fact that you saved Colomba earlier from those rocks piled on her leg." I smile at her as I stroke the feathers on her wings.

"And you're right again. You're good at this today." Shadow chuckles as she shakes her head at me.

"I can understand this. It must feel wonderful to help others with the powers you have been given."

"Yeah, especially since it was Colomba. I have a feeling that things are going to change between us now. I think that things are going to change between me and everyone in the school." She stares at me with curiosity.

"What do you mean?" I open my curtains to look out my window at the people in the street below.

"I mean that once word gets around about the Crow helping someone, people might start to think of me as the good guy too. I might get a lot of new followers from this. Who knows, I might be the one people cheer for now instead of Silver Dove."

Closing my curtains, I sit down at my desk and

pull out my sketchbook. On the second page it shows the person that I had chosen as my first soldier, Tigerclaw. I sigh softly when I look at them, feeling the failure all over again from my first attempt at helping one of the bullied kids in my school. I flip the page and start sketching on the blank paper.

"You certainly are very hopeful about this." Shadow says as my pencil carefully draws a person's leg.

"Yeah, I may have failed with the Sprinter today, but I think I have succeeded in changing a few people's minds. That is good enough for me. It's one step closer to winning this thing against Silver Dove and all the bullies in my school."

"I hope that whatever happens, it is for the best." I stop drawing for a moment to stare at Shadow.

"Don't worry, I will make sure of that." Without another word I continue to sketch in silence until I have finished. Drawn across the page is the Sprinter. She is racing across the page, determined to reach her goal. Apparently, her goal was not my goal today or else she wouldn't have stopped fighting and wouldn't have listened to Silver Dove. I suppose I can accept that though. I did win at something today. I may have turned some more people onto my side, and I think that's worth more than one small victory today.

I close my sketchbook so that I can work on a few things before going to bed. I am eager to go to school tomorrow. I can't wait to see how things will change once word gets around about what I did for Colomba. And perhaps, I may even see some change in Colomba too.

I reopen my sketchbook after I think about that. I open up to the page I had drawn the other day with myself as the Crow and me being surrounded by my loyal followers. I had left the spot beside me blank because I had wanted to put Colomba there, but I had thought that she would never want to follow me. When I think about what I did for her earlier today, I may have finally pulled her over to my side. Smiling, I sketch her standing beside me. I pay more attention to her drawing than I did for the other people in the sketch. I make her so real that it looks as if she can leap off the page. I focus mainly on her face, wanting it to be perfect. I make sure that in the picture she is smiling. She is happy to be by my side.

The smile on my face grows wider as I imagine what I will do once I have won my battle over Silver Dove and I have fixed all of the problems in my town. This will be a far more peaceful place to live once I have succeeded. People will be able to walk down the halls of my school without being afraid. They can walk down the halls with a smile on their face. I can walk down the hall with my head held high. All of the people who used to be bullies will realize that what they did was wrong, and they will be better people. Those who don't learn their lesson will be the ones picked on and bullied. They will get a taste of their own medicine. People will thank me and love me for what I have done as the Crow. More importantly, Colomba will love me for what I have done as the Crow. I will be able to walk down the hallway holding her hand without having to be afraid that Alex will do something terrible to me because of it, or worry that someone else will try and ruin my happiness. For the first time in my life I won't be afraid. I will be truly happy.

Only when I am completely satisfied with the drawing do I close the sketchbook and place it back in my desk drawer. Walking over to my laundry basket, I take out all of the clothes in it. As I start sorting some of my laundry to wash, I feel a bit of anger rise in me as I think about what Silver Dove had said. So, she pities me, does she? She thinks that she's better than me, doesn't she? What makes her think that she's so special? It's probably because everyone is cheering for her now. She thinks that she's so great because everyone thinks that she's the hero. Well she may not know it, but that's all going to change soon. Once people start to realize that I am the true hero then people will be cheering for me and not her. Soon she will be the one that is pitied. I stop sorting my laundry for a moment as I think back on my life and everything I have gone through with all of the bullies in school. Maybe I am someone that can be pitied.

My anger fades when I think of something else Silver Dove had said. She said that she isn't afraid of me anymore. Oh please, as if. No matter what she says, I don't believe her. This may have been my second failure, but I think I am getting better at this. I may also be turning Colomba onto my side. I did save her from those rocks that were pinning her leg and brought her to a safe place. Since I did that for her, she might realize that I'm not the bad guy here. Shadow seems to finally understand that too. Shadow openly said that she won't try to talk me out of this anymore, she will follow me, she is on my side.

My smile grows wider as I think about this, things are finally coming together. With Shadow truly on my side, and Colomba starting to trust me as the Crow, I may actually win this. As I finish up sorting my laundry I laugh to myself. Silver Dove was wrong. Silver Dove should be scared of me.

Chapter Twenty- One

Colomba-
Darkness Inside

We just finished eating dinner a few minutes ago. It's only eight o'clock, but I am still going to bed despite how early it is. I have had an exhausting day fighting the Sprinter and I could use all the sleep I can get, especially considering how little sleep I have been getting recently. When I place my head on the pillow and close my eyes, I expect to fall asleep immediately. I was wrong. Even though I am incredibly tired, I still can't get to sleep.

My mind is still rushing through everything that happened today. What am I going to do? How am I supposed to handle this? Now that I know that the Crow isn't such a bad guy since he saved me, things feel very different. It's going to be harder to fight him now that I know that he isn't a completely terrible person like I had seen him in my nightmares. How can I fight someone when I know that, deep down, they are a good person? It just feels so wrong. Why couldn't this have been more simple, with me fighting someone who is just plain evil? Then I wouldn't have any trouble fighting them. I could kick their butt no problem and not feel bad about it. With this, I know that I may feel guilty if I do have to face him again. He usually lets the people he has given superpowers do his dirty work for him, but this time he decided to show up himself. Who knows when he will show up again? It may be the next time or the time after that. I don't know, and that's what worries me. With the Crow, I never know what will happen.

That's not the only thing that's bothering me though. What worries me is what Megan had said to me when she revealed to me that everyone knows about how the Crow rescued me. She said that everyone thinks that I am either dating or helping the Crow, that's why he helped me. What will happen now that everyone is thinking this? Will they start hating me because of it? Will they start avoiding me because they are afraid of me? Or will they start bullying me too because they think that I'm on the same side as the Crow?

The only people who seem to support the Crow are the bullied kids in the school, but even they stay quiet about it since that would just make things worse for them. Apparently, the kids who openly tell people that they support the Crow get picked on mercilessly. I heard about one kid the other day who was openly telling people that he thinks that the Crow is doing the right thing and the next day he came into school with a black eye. He didn't tell anybody who hit him or why, but everyone already knows. Someone punched him in the eye because of what he said. I almost want to cry when I realize that I will be just like those kids. I will be picked on mercilessly since everyone will think that I am on the same side as the Crow. Everyone will hate me because of something that isn't true.

To try and calm myself, I try to think more positively. This is only a rumor. Rumors don't usually last very long, right? I'll just have to deal with this for a week, maybe even less. After that everything will get back to normal, everyone will forget about this. People will realize that I would never join sides with the Crow and they will drop all of this. They will realize that this is ridiculous. I have nothing to worry about.

I repeat these things over and over in my head, but it doesn't make the darkness inside me leave. My bad thoughts seem to poison me from the inside. My mind keeps telling me that there is no use trying to escape this. These rumors will turn everyone against me, and I can't do anything to stop it. I will be hurt because of something I didn't do.

Tears fall from my eyes and begin to soak my

pillow. I feel so lost. I don't know what to do with this. I hide my sobbing in my pillow, not wanting to disturb my father and grandmother. I can usually figure things out. I usually solve my own problems, but I can't find a way to end this. I can't change how people think. I can only hope that they will change their own minds. I know though that that will probably be impossible. Everyone will keep this lie in their heads no matter what I say. I am truly lost.

I let those thoughts fade away as I take a few deep breaths. I don't know that this will happen. I may just be making something out of nothing. All I can do is wait until morning when I go back to school, then I will find out if anything is different. For now, all I can do is sleep.

My sobs stop and my tears disappear as my eyes close softly and my mind quiets down. I drift off into sleep, but unlike how it has been lately, my nightmares do not come. For the first time in a long time, there is peace in my mind, at least while I am asleep.

Chapter Twenty- Two

Luis-
What Will
Come

As I lay down in my bed, I look up at the ceiling with a smile on my face, knowing that everything will get better from here. For the first time in my life, things are starting to look up. I close my eyes in peace while I smile to myself. This is going to be perfect. Soon nobody will be getting picked on in school because of me. I will soon be seen as the hero by everyone. Everyone will love the Crow, and Silver Dove may even join my side once she realizes that I truly am the hero. I chuckle softly to myself when I imagine what she will say when she apologizes to me for going against me for so long. I also imagine what it will sound like when Colomba admits that she was wrong about me too and that she will join the side of the Crow. I can't wait until

I hear those beautiful words. I can think of a few people who will never join my side though. That girl Angela for one, and of course Alex. Wait a minute… Alex?

I sit bolt upright in my bed, my eyes practically bugging out of my head in fear. I completely forgot about Alex. He still wants to get back at me for what I did with that mud puddle the other day. I can't even hope that he will forget about it because I know that he will never let it go until he thinks that he has punished me enough and he feels better about himself. Who knows how much he will do to me before he "forgives me" for what I have done to him? I can only imagine what he will do to me before he is satisfied. He has come up with some pretty clever punishments for me in the past.

I remember once in fifth grade, after I had accidently spilled some milk on his lap during lunch, he had come up with one of his more creative punishments. He had gone through the rest of the day as if nothing had happened, making me think that maybe I was safe, maybe he was going to let it slide. I was wrong. I was so very wrong.

The next morning, he struck when I least expected it. Every morning at our elementary school the entire school waited in front of the school before classes started and they opened the doors for us. I had been standing beside the flagpole that stood in front of the building like I did every morning. As per usual, I was standing alone since nobody would want to be seen talking with me. They would get picked on too if they were caught talking with me. While I was standing there, watching the people around me, Alex had snuck around behind me and attached my belt to the rope on the flagpole. He and a few of his other friends then hoisted me up the flagpole by the belt until I was at least fifteen feet off the ground. All of the other students looked up at me and laughed while Alex looked up at me with pride. Happy that his plan had worked so perfectly.

I was stuck up that flagpole for about ten minutes before a few teachers figured out a way to get me down safely. All during that time the other students laughed at me even though the teachers told them to stop. None of the teachers could find out if it was Alex since I hadn't actually seen him do it because he had done this from behind me and none of the other students would tell them who did it. I was everyone's punching bag by that point, so nobody really wanted to help me. Either that or they were just too scared of Alex to think about going against him and turning him in. I wouldn't blame them if they were afraid, I would have been too.

The school had sent me home early that day because of what had happened and I spent that free time alone in my room, crying my eyes out. I was devastated about what Alex had done to me and extremely embarrassed. I just wished that somebody would have stopped him, or at least help me get down instead of just laughing at me. I could have used a friend that day, but I didn't get one until this school year started when I met Colomba. I have never forgotten that incident with the flagpole. I haven't worn a belt since that day. The elementary school got rid of the flagpole after that incident, saying that they didn't want anything like that to ever happen again. If they had actually focused on the bullying instead of the stupid flagpole things might have changed for me, but of course they didn't and my life of torture from Alex continued.

I can only imagine what he will do to me now to top that. Back then I had only spilled a bit of milk on him, this time I sent him flying face first into a massive puddle of mud in front of the entire school. If he did something that bad just for a little milk, I can just tell that whatever he will do will be incredibly painful. Will he do something humiliating like with the flagpole? Or will he do something that will make me suffer?

I feel my heart tighten in my chest as I think of something. What if he does whatever he has planned in front of Colomba? What would she do if she saw him doing something to me? They share their gym class together and she considers him to be a friend. If she saw him doing something to me, would she try and help me or would she join in with whatever Alex is going to do to me?

Colomba has always been nice to me, even standing up for me against Angela when we first met, but would she side with me against Alex? Would she choose me or him? I know that practically everyone would choose Alex if they were in that situation, but Colomba isn't like everyone else. She is a good person, one of the few that I have met in our school. Maybe she would choose me because she knows that I am a good person too, unlike Alex. I don't think many people would even think of calling him a good person.

I close my eyes with my heart sinking into my chest when I realize something though. If Colomba does choose me over Alex, then she will be an outcast just like me. Alex has liked her ever since he met her too. If she chooses another guy over him then he will never forgive her. He will make sure that she will get picked on like me. Nobody will be allowed to say anything nice to her without having something bad happen to them because of Alex. He will make her life miserable, and I don't think that she can take that. She doesn't have my experience with bullying, she hasn't become numb to it like me. Colomba is a very sensitive girl. If someone were to pick on her, I don't think she could take it. If she were to get bullied like me, it would break her heart. I can't let that happen.

No matter what happens between me and

Alex, I have to make sure that Colomba isn't involved. I can't let her see what happens, I can't give her the chance to choose my side because I know what Alex will do to her if she does. She may not know what kind of a monster he is, but I do. I will protect her from him. If I have to suffer alone without her comfort to protect her, then I will be happy. No matter what Alex does to me, if she isn't involved then I will come out of it with a smile on my face.

I close my eyes again tightly in pain when I realize how I will have to do that. I will need to avoid her. I can't risk letting her see something happen to me when we hang out, so I need to stay as far away from her as possible. Until Alex makes his move against me, I will have to stay away from her. I need to stay away from the only true friend I have ever had besides Shadow. I guess, for the time being, Shadow can be my only friend.

I have been alone practically my entire life, that is until this school year started. Even though I haven't been friends with her for very long, I don't know how I can live without her friendship. It is one of the few happy things that happens during my day at school. The rest of my time at school is mainly spent trying to be invisible or avoiding other people so that people won't notice me and try to do something to me when I'm not looking. I really don't want to return to how things used to be, not even having the true friend I have in Colomba. I can already imagine how miserable it will be without her. It will be like it was before I met her, miserable and lonely, but added with the fact that I will be in more pain than ever since I will have to avoid my friend.

If Colomba can be spared the pain of having to deal with Alex, then I'm sure that everything will be alright. I can take the pain of being alone and not having her company if I know that she is happy. I would do anything to know that she is happy. My entire day, even if I have just been picked on by Alex, always seems better when I see a smile on her face. If I have to be miserable to make sure that she is happy, then I will carry that misery with me like a badge of honor.

Colomba deserves to be happy. She is always kind to everyone, no matter who they are. Even if she knows that somebody is getting picked on, she will help them, not even bothering to think about whether or not people will start picking on her too. When I think back on my life, I don't deserve to be happy like her. Whenever I think about all of the people who bully me I want to hurt them, I want to get revenge on them. I even give other bullied kids superpowers so they can get revenge. I am willing to use force to make people stop hurting each other. A person like me doesn't deserve to be happy. I guess that a person like me deserves all the bad things that happen to them. I may not deserve happiness, but I will do everything I can to make sure that Colomba is happy and safe though. If I have to suffer to make her happy then I am ready to do that for her.

Trying to make myself feel better, I remember that I do have Shadow to talk with, but that happy thought is quickly erased in my mind. Shadow can only come when I summon her, and I can only do that when I am alone. What I really want is to have someone to talk to when I am around everyone else. I don't want to have that feeling like I am alone in a crowd. That's what it feels like to me when I don't have anyone to talk to when I am in a crowded hallway. I am alone in a sea of people. Just the thought of returning to that almost makes me cry, but I hold back the tears.

I am doing this for what is best. I am doing this to protect Colomba. I just need to remember that, and I am sure that I can live through this. Repeating this over and over in my mind, I try and let my body relax so that I can get some sleep. The alarm clock beside my bed seems to tick louder and louder as I still have trouble getting to sleep. Tossing and turning, I moan to myself. Annoyed that my mind won't shut up and let me go to bed.

I open my eyes to stare at the ceiling again. I know why I can't get to sleep. My mind is trying to tell me that what I am repeating to myself is a lie. I can't just live through this like it is nothing. I have finally found a friend and now I will have to temporarily let them go so that they can be safe. There is nothing alright about that, nothing at all. I don't want to lose what little I have.

This time, I don't hold back the tears as they flow down my face. I cry that I have to do all of this. I cry that I am so pathetic and alone. I cry that I may lose the girl of my dreams and my only friend to a guy I hate. And I cry that it is all my fault. I am the one that tripped Alex and sent him flying face first into a mud puddle. I am the one that made him angry. I am the one that he wants to get revenge on. And I am the one that will have to deal with this on my own. If I want to do what is right, then I will have to live through this.

Closing my eyes again, I wait for sleep that I know will not come for a long time.

Chapter Twenty- Three

Colomba-
A Dark
New Day

I walk through the front doors of my school in a massive crowd of other students heading to their first class of the day. People bump into each other as they chat away with their friends. With everyone talking at once it creates a constant roar that seems to echo through the halls. As I walk down the hallway, even though I am alone, I smile. I'm not at all sleepy. Last night was the first time in a long time that I have had a good night's sleep without any nightmares. It was beautiful. I feel like myself again, instead of feeling like a zombie trying to make it through the school day in one piece. I am actually looking forward to the day ahead instead of dreading it like I had before. I almost feel like crying out in joy at how much better I feel.

Although I didn't have any nightmares, I did have one dream that was a bit confusing to me. In the dream I was flying through the air, but I wasn't flying because I was in my Silver Dove form. In the dream I was an actual dove. I was a little bird flying through the air on a gloriously beautiful day. I flew high in the clouds until I looked down and saw a garden that was in the courtyard of a large old building. I didn't recognize the garden, but it somehow felt as if I had been there before. I let myself fly down and land on the branch of a cherry blossom tree covered in flowers. That garden was the most beautiful place I have ever seen in my life.

Flowers were everywhere in that small garden. You could barely even see the walls of the building since it was covered by rose vines while the ground had practically every flower I could think of planted there. The air was full of the sweet scent of the flowers. I looked around with a happy heart, my eyes taking in every detail of the place, trying to memorize every detail so I could never forget that beautiful garden.

A small gravel trail that started in the large building led up to a small clearing among all the flowers. In the middle of the grass in that clearing stood a small fountain. On top of the fountain was a small statue. The statue had three people; two boys and a girl. Each of those people had a bird perched on their shoulder. One boy in the statue, who was closest to where I was perched, was tall, very thin, and had hair that hung in his face. On his shoulder he had what looked like a crow. The girl stood in the middle of the two boys. She was smaller than both of the boys and had a slightly delicate appearance. On her shoulder was what looked like a dove. The third person in the statue was harder to see since they were the farthest from me. He was tall like the other boy, but not as tall as him. He was also a bit bulkier, as if he had more muscle, a lot more than the other boy. I couldn't see what kind of bird the other boy had on his shoulder, but I could see that it was larger, much larger than the other two birds. I could not understand why, but for some reason I felt afraid yet also drawn to the final figure. Something about it fascinated me.

In the dream, I didn't bother to examine the interesting fountain any further though since something else caught my attention. I noticed that sitting on the ground beneath the swaying branches of a large weeping willow tree was a crow. The two of us stared at each other for what felt like hours, neither of us moving. The crow looked as if it wanted to come and fly to me, but it was afraid. Something in my mind told me that the crow was my enemy, but also my friend. I couldn't understand these feelings. I looked down into the crow's eyes, eyes that were so eager to see me.

Opening my tiny wings, I flew down to the crow and landed in front of it. Since I was a dove, I was so much smaller than the crow, it practically towered over me. The two of us touched beaks for a moment, almost like we were sharing a little kiss, and the crow let out a loud caw of joy. The joy didn't last though. A shadow quickly came over us and passed, as if something was flying over us. The crow looked up, its feathers fluffing out in terror as it started cawing out a warning cry. The crow hoped in front of me, spreading its wings out wide as it stared up at whatever had made that shadow. It was as if the crow was trying to protect me from whatever it was that had flown above us. I could not understand its fear, and I never got an answer to what had caused that fear because I woke up at that moment. It was a strange dream to say the least, but a good one nonetheless. After all of the horrific dreams I have been having recently, I would rather have this pleasant but confusing one than any of those other ones I've been having.

A smile is on my face at the memory of that dream as I turn around a corner. I almost stop dead in my tracks when I see a familiar face. Cheyanne is leaning up against a locker talking with a girl that I recognize from my gym class. They are laughing together, not even remotely worried about what happened yesterday with the Crow and Cheyanne becoming the Sprinter. The two of them chat as if they don't have a care in the world, the kind of conversation you can only have with a true friend. I smile as I watch the two of them, knowing that Cheyanne may have listened to the advice I gave her as Silver Dove. She might be trying to be with people who actually care about her instead of just for the way she can run and win tournaments for the school. The girl Cheyanne is talking to gives her a quick goodbye before heading down the hall while Cheyanne walks in the opposite direction to probably head to her next class.

I watch Cheyanne as she walks down the hall on her newly healed leg. As I watch her walk away from me, some of the friends she had on the team who ended up ditching her when she was hurt try to get close to her. They gather around her and act as if what happened yesterday didn't happen. They all smile at her and try to talk as if they had never done any of those horrible things they did only just the other day. My body grows tense as I wait to see what will happen, worried that she will fall for their lies again, worried that she will try to be friends with the very people who hurt her. I don't have to worry about Cheyanne though, she knows that they are just being nice to her because she will be the best on the team again with her healed leg. Cheyanne doesn't believe their lies anymore. She gives them a simple goodbye before she walks away from them, knowing that they are not her true friends. They never were.

I smile when I see this, knowing that she has truly learned her lesson. Cheyanne walks past me without really seeing me. Not realizing that she is walking past the person who helped her yesterday, the one who healed her leg. I don't feel bad about this though. I don't expect to be praised for what I did. I am just happy that things have worked out well for her and that she is now heading down a path that will be better for her in the long run. I continue to walk down the hallway to head to class, but my smile begins to fade when I overhear someone saying something that grabs my attention.

"She's the one that I saw getting carried by the Crow the other day when the Sprinter was attacking the school."

"Are you sure?"

"Definitely. I bet she's helping him in some way. That's why he helped her when those rocks fell on her."

"You're probably right. She always acts like such a perfect little lady, I bet it's all an act so that nobody suspects her. She's probably plotting with the Crow to help him with his next attack."

I look over to my side to see a guy who quickly lowers his hand and looks away from me. The person who he had been talking to looks away as well while I can see a blush forming on their cheeks. I know why he put his hand down, he had been pointing at me. Judging from the way he was talking about that, he does not approve of the Crow helping me. I also know that this gossip will be spread throughout the school by the end of the day. Everyone will know. My heart sinks in my chest and my mouth goes dry. How will the rest of the school react to this news?

I almost feel like crying when the obvious answer pops into my head. Because of this news spreading throughout the school the next bullied kid that the Crow will try to "help" might just be me. I hurry down the hall, wanting to escape from that boy I had heard talking about me. I practically run through the crowd, but it doesn't feel like I'm going fast enough.

I fight back the tears that threaten to fall down my face. I won't let this beat me. I can only try to make myself not feel hurt by this so that the Crow won't be tempted to possess me like he has already done to Tigerclaw and the Sprinter. I can't let myself be seen as the victim or the bullied kid. As I hurry down the hallway to get to my next class I keep repeating in my mind that I just need to keep a positive attitude and everything will be alright. I keep saying this, but the tears still threaten to come. Even though I am surrounded by countless people I feel so alone. I am all alone in the world.

Eliza Scalia is currently a Masters student for Clinical Mental Health at Troy University. She enjoys reading and needlework, as well as hanging out with her pet cat, Dusty. Eliza has been writing for many years and has self- published the Death's Assistant series for young adults.